THE MAW OF MAYHEM

A MAW OF MAYHEM SHIFTER MC PREQUEL

AK NEVERMORE

CONTENTS

CATS DON'T ALWAYS LAND ON THEIR FEET...

Grimdarke James has got problems. As Vice Prez of the Maw of Mayhem MC, he needs to keep his shit together, but between the constant threat of his inner cat going feral again, and Nikki, one of the motorcycle club's mollys, blackmailing him, it's a fine line some days.

When an arms deal goes bad, everything goes to hell with it. All fingers point to an old club enemy, a man Grim has reason to both fear and loathe, but the facts don't add up, and everyone is a suspect... even him. Faced with the constant threat of Nikki revealing his past and his need to prove himself to the MC, the fragile peace he's made with his cat is threatened.

Out of options and running out of time, Grim sets a bold plan into motion, and the consequences are far more dire than he could have imagined...

A HEADS UP ON CONTENT

Don't try this stuff at home. This book explores themes which some readers may find uncomfortable or offensive. If violence, smut, various kinks, salty language, drug use, and generally unsavory behavior are triggers for you, please put this novella down and back away slowly.

CHAPTER ONE

GRIM'S fingers ghosted over the butt of his gun, eyes on the long sinuous shadow of a lynx stalking from one patch of darkness to another. It was one of their crew, but Christ, this arms deal, just east of butt-fuck, had the nape of his neck prickling. Goddamned hills surrounding the warehouse were too quiet, and the fact that the rest of the MC's men were skulking around out there in cat form had nothing to do with it.

Drop shouldn't be taking this long.

[UNEASE]

His inner cat paced, tail flicking, and damn if he didn't feel like doing the same.

"Something's off," he murmured.

"Clay has it handled," the brother at his right replied, glancing at his phone, too bright in the moonlight. "Vans just cleared the bridge. Some shit about a flat. ETA five minutes."

A fucking flat? Since when did an entire convoy stop for one downed vehicle? Grim flicked his eyes from the road below to MK. The MC's road captain was too damned calm.

"I don't like it."

MK snorted. "You don't like anything."

He had a point, but fuck him. Grim kicked at an outcropping of stone, sending scree rattling down the hillside. Fuck that, too. MK wasn't worried, why should he be? Down in the valley, headlights sparked into view on the winding road, flickering through the trees. Five sets, following ass to nose.

"That'll be them," MK said, shoving his phone in his pocket. "Tell that cunt cat of yours to calm down. This deal's too big for him to fuck up."

—growling—

Yeah, but he's not wrong, and you've been a miserable prick lately. Fuck, maybe that's why he was so on edge. With all the shit going sideways with their supply routes the past few weeks, Grim couldn't remember the last time he'd let the furry fucker out.

Oh wait, yeah, he could. He was still picking bits of blood off his bike.

[ANGER]

It's your own damned fault. His cat's impulse control was for shit on a good day, and this wasn't one of them. "He won't be an issue."

MK shot him a look that said he'd believe it when he'd seen it. And that was the problem right there. Too many of the brothers didn't trust him to keep his shit together.

Neither did he.

Grim took a deep breath, fingers raking through his shaggy blond hair. Jesus Fuck, it shouldn't be this goddamned hard. Clay believed in him, had made him his VP for a reason, despite all the pushback from the club—

Whatever. He sighed, staring up at the moon and wishing —Fuck what he was wishing. Shit never worked anyway. He had to take tonight for what it was; another chance to prove he deserved his patch.

And he'd be damned if he let Clay down.

Especially with the problems the last two shipments of arms had run into. They couldn't afford to have this one go off the rails because of Grim's cat or anything else, which is why they had a full crew out here. Their supplier was getting nervous, and word on the street was they were looking into other distributors. That meant one of two things; either the cartel was gonna run the risk of transporting over Niagara, or they were gonna back Satan's Vengeance MC to take over their territory.

Grim knew where his money was. The Niagara route was way too fucking dicey, and the cartel's backing was exactly the opportunity those SV bastards had been praying for to push the Maw of Mayhem out of St. Lawrence County. Assholes had a hard on for them even before they'd gotten SV's piece of shit alpha locked up.

Gravel crunched and high beams swung across the warehouse's bay doors, dust and detritus swirling through the sudden shock of light. Grim looked away, trying to preserve his night vision.

Which is when he saw it.

The quick pulse of LED red, deep in the third van's rear wheel well as it humped over a rut. The fuck? Grim started forward, and MK clotheslined him, blocking his progress.

"Didn't you see that?" Grim hissed.

"See what? You about to blow our position?" MK spat back with a sneer. "Yeah. Why do you think Clay's got me babysitting your ass out here on the fringe? You're a fucking liability—"

"No, asswipe, the tech mounted to the third van," he gritted out past his hurt. "They got some shit rigged—"

"Why the fuck would Cantone mess with his own shipment? Man's already paid a mint for what's in those crates. Probably just one of them gangbangers pimpin' out his cage."

Grim ran a hand over his jaw, shaking his head. MK was right about Cantone, but the rest of it? Who the fuck tricked out a laundry truck? Nah. Shit wasn't sittin' right.

The vans came to a halt, and the warehouse's bay door rumbled upwards. More men than they'd expected exited the vehicles, engines still running. Clay walked out to meet them, hands in his pockets. He paused, then pulled out a toothpick and rolled it to the side of his mouth.

Grim smacked MK's arm away, jerking his head at their alpha's signal for impending fuckery. "See, asswipe?" Clay knew something was off too. MK's lips tightened.

"Thought Espada was on this run," Clay said like he didn't give a fuck.

A burly man in a skullcap shrugged. "You got me instead. Where's our shit?"

"Depends. Where's the rest of my money?"

The breeze picked up, redolent with exhaust and motor oil. Grim's brow furrowed, his lip curling, canines extending. Scenting the air he drew into his mouth… Fuck. He spat the taste from his mouth, eyeing the vans. Make that a shit ton of motor oil with a side of nasty-ass BO. The kind humans put out when they were shitting themselves about something, and in the unlikely event one of those cages was pissing out that much lube, it would've been smoking like a moth-erfucker.

Yeah. It wasn't motor oil he was scenting; it was C-4.

[RAGE RAGE RAGE]

No shit, but—

—Clay!—

His cat's consciousness slammed into his, and Grim went rigid, locking down his body's overwhelming desire to shift, fighting the slide of muscle and bone—

No, you fucker, not—

"Goddamn it!" MK hissed, lunging at him.

The cat abruptly retreated, and before Grim could get his bearings, the furry fuck used his mouth to chirp out the club's cry for betrayal.

Brothers dove for cover. Bangers yelled, drawing their guns and pointing into the darkness as they backed toward their vehicles, deal totally fucked.

"You stupid shit," MK swore, grabbing Grim by his cut and slamming him—

The night exploded into a raging ball of fire.

The blast blew them apart and into the bracken, thorns tearing across Grim's flesh, air knocked from his lungs as he hit—

—KILL!—

His cat exploded outward, fabric shredding and joints popping, completing its shift mid-stride. The mountain lion hit one of the bangers drawing a bead on a brother, snapping his neck and grinding his face into the gravel with one huge paw—

A line of fire blazed across his shoulder and he hunched down, growling in the direction it'd come from. Another bullet zinged past, and he took off running. The blast had scattered the convoy like matchbox cars, the front of the ware-house twisted and blackened.

—Clay!—

Grim's cat sprinted behind an overturned vehicle, gun shots ringing out. A lynx yowled and men screamed, the sounds of carnage drowning out the roar and crackle of flames. Clay and another brother were behind one of the crates, popping off rounds.

He's fine, you fuck!

[RAGE RAGE RAGE]

Let me out!

—NO—

Grim panted, trying to take back control. *Darke!* The cat ignored him, shoving him back into the recesses of their mind, while he mercilessly stalked his prey.

There was blood.

Long ropes of viscera sizzling in the flames where they'd been flung, the coppery mineral tang dripping from his jaws. His path of destruction mapped with gore-soaked prints and chunks of mauled flesh. The screams of the enemy echoing through the night, their bodies left disemboweled and steaming, scattered and broken throughout the late summer woods.

Moments stretched, stars rising on the horizon. Men fell. Running from their deaths. Darke found them, one by one, snuffing out their light.

The last cowered behind a low stone wall, wide-eyed and trembling, his own gun cocked beneath his chin. Darke growled from the shadows and the banger let out a shriek, the scent of piss souring the air.

"I-I didn't fucking know, man... I didn't fucking know!" He sobbed, snot running from his nose. Grim's cat took a half a step forward, purposefully cracking a dead branch beneath his massive paw with a low growl.

Darke, you shit, stop fucking with him.

—laughing—

The banger clenched the gun tighter, his eyes screwing shut. "I don't—I don't w-wanna die..."

Christ, just put this pussy out of his misery...

—keeping him—

Why, you run out of catnip mice?

Darke chuffed, a red mist spraying from his nostrils, and the banger went limp, eyes rolling up into his head.

Was it a game? The cat's head cocked, waiting for him to move.

No. The mother fucker fainted. Drag his ass back to Clay.

—boring—

You wanted to keep him. Darke huffed and bit into the banger's jacket, dragging him through the woods.

Clay was with part of the crew in front of the warehouse, filthy as fuck, but unharmed. He ran a hand down his soot-streaked face, listening to one of the brothers report.

Darke had been out hunting long enough for them to set up floodlights and start clearing shit. Heaps of twisted metal and glass glittered like the place had been decorated for a goth prom, burning tires and a cannibal's barbecue flavoring the air. The cat picked around the debris, a lot less selective about what he towed the banger through.

"Good, you kept one to play with," Clay said when they got close.

—see—

Whatever. Let me out so I can deal with this shit, Grim grumbled, well aware that Clay's expression was more relieved to see him than it should've been. Shame churned through his gut at the likelihood they'd all thought he'd gone feral again.

Darke retreated, and Grim's body reformed to stand beside his alpha, skin stippled and smeared with viscera. He spat the mineral funk from his mouth. Goddamn, people tasted like shit. Clay handed him a flask. The brothers he'd been talking to smelled nervous and wouldn't look his way.

Par for the fucking course.

"When Doc gets here, get her to take a look at that," Clay said, eyeing the ragged wound across Grim's shoulder. "Brick, why don't you go make our guest comfortable."

The MC's enforcer separated himself from another group, smirking. He threw the banger over his massive shoulder like a bag of laundry and tromped into the warehouse. Pansy shit wasn't gonna do well down in the vault.

Oh fucking well.

Grim watched them go, almost feeling sorry the pussy.

Almost.

He tipped back the flask. His shoulder throbbed, but not as bad as it would after Doc had her way with it. Might as well self-medicate while he could. He ignored the side-eye he was getting from the brothers. Even the ones he called friends went on edge when his cat came out. Clay said it was because they shifted to smaller cats—lynxes to his mountain lion—but that was bullshit. No one batted an eye when the alpha's beast came out... but then they trusted Clay to keep a leash on his shit.

Darke wasn't exactly a team player, and a couple of them had the scars to prove it.

—deserved it—

No, you're just a dick. Grim sighed, taking another swig, his fingers leaving sticky crimson smears on the flask. "How bad we get hit?"

Clay scratched his bearded jaw. "Not terrible, considering. MK got the worst of it. Shrapnel from one of them cages fucked his leg up royal, and the man's out cold. Deuce's gonna need stitches, Wrench took a bullet, rest of it—" He shrugged. "You made a good call. What tipped you off?"

"Saw LEDs in the wheel well." Grim picked at the rusty half-moons beneath his nails, Clay's silence telling him he was waiting for the rest of it. "Stank like oil," he muttered so the rest of the brothers couldn't hear. "Too much."

His alpha's lips pursed. "Being able to use your cat's senses while you're on two legs ain't something to be ashamed of, son. It saved our asses tonight."

Grim frowned, still picking at his nails. Maybe. But it wasn't fucking natural, or a point in his favor as far as the rest of the shifter community was concerned. Just another reason no one trusted him or his damned cat.

Furry fucker still preened.

"They found Espada floating about an hour ago." Clay said. "His crew's missing, along with the rest of our cash. Cantone's out for fucking blood."

Yeah, that tracked. Grim took another swallow of booze, then licked across his teeth and spat out a chunk of offal. Tasted like liver. Shit was disgusting. "Merchandise?"

"One crate's fucked. Rest are good, but we're gonna have to eat the loss to keep the contract…" He looked past Grim's shoulder, toward the road. Headlights bobbed. "That'll be Doc and the other crew. Go clean up. Brothers found what was left of your shit when they brought back MK. It's in the bunk."

Grim nodded, handing him the empty flask, pretending not to see Clay frowning at the rusty smears marring its surface.

He beat a hasty retreat into the warehouse.

Aside from the bay door being blown in and that mangled crate, the rest of the merchandise sat untouched, stacked in the center of the cavernous space. Along the back wall, a row of office pods had been converted into a bunkhouse.

Grim trudged into the showers and flicked on the spray. Damn it. Water wasn't totally glacial, but it was close. He grabbed the lava soap and sluiced off the gore, water running a gritty red, then pink, bits of banger becoming fewer and farther in between.

By the time it ran clear, the last vestiges of hot water were gone and the soreness from his rapid shift had set in, friction burns from bursting through his clothes stinging. He grabbed a towel, making a beeline to the pile of his shredded belongings.

Jeans, shirt, and his cut were all fucked. Goddamn it—

—suck it up—

Fuck you. How about some warning next time? I hate it when you do that.

[SMUG]

—saved Clay—

Yeah… maybe.

—did—

Don't let it go to your head.

—chuffing—

Grim frowned, too fucking late for that. He toweled off and grabbed a pair of sweats and a T from supply. At least the furry fuck had managed to kick out of his boots before ruining those, too. Guess the last time he'd left them limping for a couple of weeks had taught him a lesson. *Yes, folks, he can be trained—*

—fuck you—

You do. Constantly.

—grumbling—

Grim pocketed his wallet and keys. Phone. The fuck if he knew what he was gonna do with his gun… Sighing, he tied the drawstring of his sweats tight and slipped it into his waistband. Going without it seemed fucking stupid. He stepped into his boots and tossed the T over the shoulder that wasn't dribbling crimson down his arm, heading back out to find Doc. He pulled up short at her voice just outside the bunk's door.

"…him or his cat?"

"Dunno…" Clay blew out a breath. "I had MK sitting on him, but he ain't in any condition to report."

"Won't be for a while." Doc's voice grated, pure bitch. "Digging out all that shattered bone's above my pay grade. You need to send him to Union General, or hire a witch. Even then, there's no guarantee he'll walk, never mind ride again with his femur that fucked."

Clay grunted. "Do what you gotta—"

"How long was he out?"

Shit. Doc was asking about Grim's cat. There was a pregnant pause, and he started to sweat.

"Little over an hour," Clay finally said. "Crew left him the runners. He dragged one of them back alive, but I'm guessing the rest of them ain't."

Doc snorted. "There's no guessing about it. I don't know what the fuck you were thinking leaving your kid with Reaper for so goddamned long, but Grim's his fucking protege—"

Clay growled. "Grim's nothing like Reaper."

"Carnage his cat leaves says otherwise."

And there was that fucking silence again. Grim put a hand to the wall, head hanging as he bit at his lips. Woman was right. Way Darke dealt out death was the one damned thing about him his adopted "uncle" had approved of.

Until he'd refused to do it anymore.

He grimaced at the memory of silver biting into his flesh. Shit hadn't gone over well, and what'd come after was worse. Especially since his defying Reaper hadn't achieved anything; then or now.

Grim's chest ached. He was never gonna get out from under that psycho's fucking shadow, and not even Clay, his father by blood, could say otherwise. The stain of being raised by Reaper would follow Grim to his grave.

His fist clenched. Why hadn't Clay claimed him sooner? Wasn't the first time he'd asked himself that question, and it wouldn't be the last. He was too chickenshit to corner his dad on the subject; equal parts doubtful he'd get an answer and terrified he would.

His father let out a long breath. "All that fury's gonna serve him well. Something's coming. Witches, vamps... too much is in flux. This tonight, issues with the other runs... it's all part and parcel. I need the MC to back him."

"And I need a bathing suit that's both comfortable and flattering. Even odds who gets their wish first. Look, fuck all that doom-speak for a minute. Boy's not stable, and if he goes feral again—"

"He won't. Can't. I need him."

But he had. Not two fucking hours ago. Damn cat had taken control and run rampant.

—let you back—

This time.

—laughing—

Doc snorted, and Grim ripped open the door, tired of listening to their shit. Clay met his eyes with a look that said he knew Grim'd heard the whole thing. Doc just looked pissed, but the acerbic older woman always did.

Her glare fell on his shoulder. "The fuck you do to yourself now?"

Grim didn't bother to answer, gaze still locked with Clay's.

Doc frowned at them, the lines on her brow etching deep as she crouched to root through her med kit. "Tell me you were in control of the shift."

He couldn't.

Instead, he shrugged, turning from his father and trying to play it off. "Wasn't an issue."

"This time." Her mouth set into a thin white line. "Sit your ass down so I can sew you up," she said, pointing to the floor. "Last thing I need is you passing out and giving yourself a goddamned concussion."

He lowered himself down, setting his piece to the side and sitting with his back against the wall. "I don't pass out."

Doc eyed the gun. "First time for everything, even with your freakish tolerance for pain," she muttered, liberally swabbing him down with something that burnt like a motherfucker.

"Head back to the club with Deuce and Wrench when she's finished," Clay said, hands in his pockets. "I've got clean up and some words for our guest. Plan on meeting with the rest of the table first thing."

Grim nodded, gritting his teeth. Stars exploded across his vision as Doc scraped out the wound, hell-bent on testing her theory about him passing out. Cold sweat pebbled his skin, stomach roiling by the time she was through.

"Got any rock salt to grind into it? Think you missed a spot," he muttered. Shit throbbed so bad it had its own heartbeat.

Doc's lips quirked, inspecting the needle from her suture kit. "I'll remember that for next time." She jabbed him and started stitching.

Grim grunted at the steady stab and pull through his flesh, the burn of it inching over his shoulder, wound closing up in its wake. She smeared it with goo when she was done and taped on a bandage.

"Leave it the fuck alone. I'll send Triss by to check on it tomorrow."

He bit back his sigh of relief as he stood, jamming his piece back into his waistband. Triss's bedside manner was a hell of a lot more palatable, short term at least. Girl was too fucking cheery for her own good. How she was Doc's daughter was a mystery. Grim tugged on his shirt, wincing. Half-hour ride back to the clubhouse was gonna suck.

Deuce and Wrench were at the back of the warehouse, laughing and sharing a smoke. He nodded at the two, going to his bike. Despite their good humor, Wrench was favoring a leg and Deuce's hand was bandaged up just shy of a mitten.

"Grim, you savage motherfucker!" Deuce howled, coming over and smacking him on the back. "That was fucking epic! Them bangers didn't know what hit 'em. You shoulda heard the one you dragged in crying when his pansy ass woke up and saw Brick. I kid you not, the dude literally shit himself."

"True story," Wrench added, flicking away his butt. "He's down there selling out everyone, including his mom. Guess the bitch sells bootleg Hallmark DVDs. Brick's fucking pissed. You know he likes to work at makin' them sing. The fuck you do to the dude?"

[SMUG]

Grim shrugged. "I dunno. Found him holding his own gun to his head. Probably new meat. All of 'em scattered like it was every man for himself. I'd be surprised if they'd run together before tonight."

"Ah ah…" Deuce tapped his temple and smirked at Grim. "Careful. Keep talking like that, people'll think there's brains behind that miserable exterior."

"Fuck you."

The brothers both laughed, echoing Grim's bitch ass cat, and mounted their bikes. The motion wiped the humor off

Wrench's face, his pug nose scrunching up as he winced. "Fucking fuck. This is gonna blow."

"So are the mollys when we get back to the club. First one I see better be on her knees."

Grim had no doubt one of the club-slut shifters would be. Deuce was GQ in a cut.

Wrench snorted at him. "Even if it's Triss?"

"You watch your fucking mouth," the brother snapped, jabbing his mitten at him. "Triss ain't a slut."

Wrench grinned at him, buckling his dome. "Nope. But she's got one fine ass—"

"You want yours beat?" Deuce growled. "I swear to Christ, if you're fuckin' with her—"

"He's just being a dick," Grim said, wheeling his bike backward. "Everyone knows she's off-limits. Why you're not tapping that…"

"She's too fucking young."

"She doesn't think so."

"Not helpful," Deuce glared at him. "And ain't you got enough on your plate with Nikki there, Grimmers?"

He couldn't stop himself from cringing at the inane nickname he'd been saddled with. His dickhead friends laughed, and he just shook his head, pushing up to kickstart his bike and swearing at the burn in his shoulder.

"That'll teach ya to join this century, asshole!" Deuce's bike rumbled on with the push of a button, and Wrench's followed suit.

"Fuck you, it's a classic." Bastards wished they had a Bobber.

"So's my granny, but ain't nobody riding her!" Deuce laughed, peeling out of the lot on his hog. Wrench and Grim trailed in his wake down the winding mountain roads.

Grim lagged behind the other two, not in any hurry to get back to the clubhouse. That, and he kept having to drop his arm after he shifted. Fucking shoulder was killing him. He was probably fifteen minutes behind them when he finally rode through the clubhouse gates with a nod to the abundance of armed prospects on duty. Good call. There was always the chance whoever had set them up would take the fallout from tonight as an opportunity to hit the club.

Especially if it'd been Satan's Vengeance. Assholes had raided the compound years back, and the dirty fuckers had no issue taking out women and kids. Clay had lost his ol' lady and adopted daughter in the raid.

The bad blood between the two MCs ran deep.

The prospects rolled the chain link closed behind him, locking up for the night.

Clean up at the warehouse wasn't gonna be quick, and it needed to be done right. Clay had most of the law looking the other way, but if someone dropped a dime about what'd gone down earlier… Feds would be all over that like stink on shit.

Grim rounded the bend in the road and the woods opened up. The clubhouse was in the center of a razed clearing, cinderblock walls stark in the moonlight. Windows blazed with light and Kid Rock's *American Badass* was blasting behind the walls. Typical Friday night in full swing.

Grim's bike backfired as he downshifted, parking at the end of the row with a sigh. Jets needed to be replaced weeks ago. Shit was running lean, and he wasn't doing his engine any favors.

Whatever. Parts had come in a couple of days ago, and it wasn't like he had anything else to do after table met. He left his dome on the seat and stomped up the steps, riffling his hair. Pushed through the door. Music blared louder and laughter assaulted him. Air thick with mating pheromones and stale beer. Deuce was on the couch with a molly busy between his legs. He raised his beer at Grim and grinned. Man wasn't one to waste time, that was for sure.

Wrench was at the bar, and Grim took the stool beside him, pausing to appreciate another molly spread out a few seats down, a brother's face buried between her legs. Club whore's tits were on point. She pulled at them, moaning.

Hanna, one of the ol' ladies, came over with his usual three fingers of Jack, frowning at the display.

"Not into the show?" he asked, tossing it back.

She refilled his glass, lips pursed. "Shit's unsanitary. People eat up here."

"Apparently." Grim deadpanned.

Hanna glowered at him, thumping the bottle down and leaving. What the hell was her problem?

"Careful, man," Wrench said, snagging it to top off his drink. "You don't need her pissed at you."

"Why would she be pissed at me?"

" 'Cause Nikki's the reason the ol' ladies and the mollys have been going at it lately."

[ANGER]

"The fuck she do now?"

Wrench looked at him like he was stupid, and Grim's mouth curdled. Better question was what hadn't she done to get under their skin. Woman was always fucking pushing for more. More attention, more privileges, more—

"Grimmers!" He grunted as a pair of fake-ass tits slammed into his back. Speak of the damned devil. Nikki's arms wrapped around his torso. He tensed, his cat's proverbial tail lashing. Beast hated the bitch.

It was one of the few things they agreed on.

—cum slut—

"Are you okay? They said you were shot!" Her saccharine shrill voice cut through the music, even the molly getting her pussy licked glanced over at them.

Center stage, exactly what Nikki wanted.

Grim turned, peeling her off him and settling the bottle in his lap to keep her out of it. "I'm fine."

Her big blue eyes widened, going to the line of red seeping through his T. Damn. The ride home hadn't done him any favors. She reached towards it, playing the sympathetic girlfriend to a tee. Grim jerked back.

—growling—

"Leave it."

"But—"

"Doc said not to fuck with it."

Her plump plum lips flattened. No love lost between those two. Probably because Nikki had fucked Stitch, Doc's ol' man, right after she'd gotten up here. "I was worried."

—lie—

Grim snorted. Not exactly, but it sure as hell wasn't the truth. He tipped the bottle back, abruptly needing a hell of a lot more alcohol than what would fit in his glass. "Were you now." Shit wasn't a question, and he didn't give a fuck what her answer was.

Nikki fiddled with a long blonde lock, twisting it around her fingers like a threat. Damn. All that nastiness wrapped up in a pretty, pretty package. There was no denying she was smokin' hot, and the china blue lace teddy she was wearing hugged her manufactured curves like it'd been made for her.

Maybe it'd come with those tits the last time she'd added a cup size.

She pushed between his knees, her hands on his thighs, lavender manicure sinking possessively into his flesh. "You know I hate it when you go out on runs." She batted too-long lashes, her face angelic.

And totally full of shit.

—growling—

He took another pull off the bottle. "You know I don't care."

"You should." Malice sparked in those baby blues, and Grim's knuckles went white around the neck of the bottle. Her hand snaked around his nape, pulling his face close to hers. "Especially if you want to keep certain conditions private…" she murmured, glancing at his lap before and licking her lips.

Grim's stomach dropped. She wanted to give the room a show, and one way or another, was gonna.

How long had it been since his last forced performance? Fuck it. He'd had just enough booze not to care. His arm caged her waist, jerking her against him. He dipped his head to nuzzle behind her ear, his canines elongating. It would be so damned easy to tear out her throat…

—DO IT—

No. Just laying hands on a molly would get him lynched, never mind killing one. No matter how much she deserved it.

Or how much he'd enjoy it. Shit played out in his head, so real he could feel the hot spatter of her bleeding out. His dick twitched.

—YESSS—

"You fucking disgust me." Grim breathed into her ear like a lover. The seat beside them skidded back and Wrench clapped him on the shoulder, leaving them to it.

Nikki laughed, watching him go. "That's what makes this so much fun." She pulled away to boop Grim's nose, and he growled, stool falling back as he shot to his feet and pinned her against the bar. Her eyes sparkled and the scent of her arousal thickened the air.

Bitch was baiting him.

[ANGER]

Grim loomed over her, forcing her backwards until she was supine across the bar, her legs around his waist. She wanted to give the room a show? Yeah, he'd give 'em a fucking show. A brother whistled as Grim captured her wrists, ignoring the pain in his shoulder, and jerking them above her head. Catcalls rained down around them, and Nikki purred beneath the attention, her back arching up off the bar top.

"This what you want? For everyone to see what a dirty whore you are?"

"Mmm, I want them to see I'm *your* dirty whore, Grimmers." She squirmed her hips against him, panting.

"You're not my anything," he murmured, his shaggy hair hiding his disdain as he eyed the rapid rise and fall of her tits, nipples peaked against the lace. He grabbed a scant handful of cloth and she gasped.

"No, wait don't—"

He tore the teddy away, chuckling at her screech. Brothers clapped, laughing.

"You fucking asshole! I—"

He slapped her tit. Shit barely moved, but she gasped, moaning at the cruel pinch to her nipple, the heat at her core soaking through his T, sloppy against his abs. His thumb dropped to circle her clit, and she groaned, rocking into his touch. "You what?"

"Want you. So bad. Oh, please, just like this, Grimmers, fuck me…"

[DISGUST]

Yeah. Wasn't happening, no matter how much she begged for it. If his dick could've crawled inside him, it would've. And even if he had wanted it, his cat wouldn't allow it.

Not after all the shit Reaper had made them do. Sex was off the table.

And somehow, Nikki knew every sordid detail. Her calling him out to bang her in front of the crowd, fully aware of what making him do shit to her did to him, to his cat… his shame was what she got off on.

And the bitch was fucking soaked.

[ANGER]

Grim traced her sopping slit, and she whimpered, hips jerking for more. He slipped a finger inside her folds, pumping. She writhed worthy of a porno, her walls fluttering, sucking at him like a leech. The brothers around them were intent on the performance, cocks tenting their jeans. Hands rubbing across their lips, drinks emptying faster.

Grim's cat had retreated to the far reaches of his consciousness, and he just felt fucking dirty. Goddamn, was keeping her mouth shut really worth it?

If the brothers wanted her, they could fucking—

—Clay—

Grim's chest tightened. *Yeah.* That's why he'd agreed to this fucked up deal with Nikki. His father could never find out what he'd done. Shit would kill him.

But right about now? This almost seemed worse.

Nauseated, Grim withdrew his hand, leaving Nikki on the brink. She cried out, her brow furrowed with need. His cat growled at the salty tang of her arousal coating Grim's fingers.

—cum slut—

Grim frowned, smelling it too. Bitch had just bent over for someone. He shoved his sticky fingers into her mouth.

"Suck 'em, you filthy slut."

She complied with a remorseless moan.

God, he fucking hated her. This. His temper spiked, teeth gnashing. "You really think I'd fuck you when you're full of someone else's cum?" Her pupils blew out, and she panted. Grim shook his head at the nasty bitch. He went to push away from her, and she fisted his T, lips close to his ear.

"I'd never think that," she whispered. "Since you can't get it up with a woman, I'd planned on making you eat it."

Her eyes locked on his, pure fucking depravity in their depths. She tongued a too-pointy canine, smirking.

—KILL—

Grim focused his rage and slapped her pussy. She yelped, breath coming fast.

"I don't tom around, Nikki," he said, pitching his voice so the voyeurs could listen in. "And I don't want a molly for my queen. If you're gonna fuck brothers like the rest of the club-sluts, we're done."

"I—" Nikki glanced at their audience, her bottom lip jutting out and trembling. "Please, Grimmers, I won't do it again, I'll be good, I'll—"

"Did you wanna make me jealous? Is that it?" He snorted. "Fuck one of 'em right now. See if I care."

—laughing—

Heads turned and the conversation in the room dropped, music thumping louder in its absence. Nikki's eyes flashed, and he stepped back, arms over his chest. She sat up on the bar, crossing her long legs and swinging a foot. Totally blasé that her tits were hanging out and she was perched in a puddle of Jack.

"Well?" Grim scanned the room. "Any takers? Don't be shy, she's fucking primed to pump. I know plenty of you have already been tapping that. Mack? Happy?" The two grizzled brothers shook their heads, shuffling their beat-to-shit boots. Couple of fucking catches right there. "No? How 'bout you, Wallace? No? Huh." Grim turned back to Nikki. Bitch was fuming.

"Ah shit, I'm sorry. I shoulda asked you first. Which brother were you gonna fuck behind my back next? You probably got a checklist to keep things tidy."

"You're a fucking asshole." She hopped off the bar and stood with her hands on her hips.

"And you're nothing but a run-of-the-mill molly lifting her tail for any brother looking for a wet hole. You wanna be a queen? Act like one."

He stormed out of the club's bar, heart pounding, the clack of her stilettos chasing him down. "Grim! Wait!"

Fuck that. He hit the stairs to the bunks and climbed them two at a time, his stride leaving her in the dust.

"Grim!"

He paused at the landing, jaw clenched. A molly came out

of one of the rooms, eyebrows raised in interest. Nope. Wasn't doing this with an audience. He stomped past her to his room at the end of the hall, punching in his code and throwing the door open.

Nikki's fists hit the other side just as it snicked shut. He latched the chain, not putting it past her to have his code.

"Grim! We need to talk about this!"

No, they needed to fucking end this. He raked a hand through his hair and leaned against the windowsill, looking out. More pounding on the door. He didn't care. Goddamn, his life was shit. Between the constant threat of his cat going feral again and this twisted deal with Nikki, it was no wonder the entire MC thought he was a fuckup. He couldn't keep either of them in line, how did he expect to earn the brothers' respect?

Outside, the night called to him, to his cat.

—cave—

Sleeping dirt sounded better than it should've. Shifting would pop his stitches, but he wasn't sure he cared. Grim winced, stripping off his T. Every damned muscle in his torso protested, that rapid shift earlier had beat him the fuck up. He moved to sit on the edge of the bed, then fell back on the mattress with a groan. As much as he wanted to run away, his body wanted to be in bed more. He emptied the shit from his pockets and dumped it on his nightstand along with his gun. Traded that for the half a pint of Jack in the drawer.

"Grim!" Nikki's voice had gone from pleading to pissed.

He kicked off his boots. Snagged his headphones from the bedpost and shoved them on; Seether drowning her out as he scrolled through his phone.

Clay had texted. Clean up was going well. Someone had tipped off the PD about the blast, but Clay had explained it away as a drunken fireworks mishap. Sheriff wasn't coming out until the morning. Bodies should be clear by then.

The banger Grim has dragged back was currently giving

them shit on his elementary school teachers and a bunch of other useless crap. Salient points? Grim had been right about them not working together before, and Brick had gotten a name. Mouse, their tech wiz, was already on it.

club good?

Grim's thumb hovered over his father's last text message.

No, things were shit, but—he sent a thumbs up.

Clay hit him right back with an eye roll gif. *after table you're lysoling the bar.*

Damn. Grim snorted and tossed the phone down. Club gossip spread faster than VD. He scrubbed at his face—

The door slammed open against the chain, and he sighed, pulling off his headphones.

—*growling*—

"Let. Me. In."

"Mouse give you the code after you blew him?"

"Stop being such a fucking asshole!" She hissed through the crack, rattling the chain like a bitchy Jacob Marley. "Open the damned door, Grim."

He sighed, throwing his legs over the side of the bed and wincing. Fuck, he hurt. "What d'you want?"

"We need to talk about this."

"I got nothing to say. You've fucked my reputation along with every brother downstairs." Grim scratched at his jaw as he stood. "Shit, maybe it's better this way. Once someone else is wearing the VP patch, you won't have any use for me, will you?"

Shit, maybe that was the answer. Go nomad. Leave all this behind him.

—*Clay*—

Grim frowned, not needing his dumbass cat to remind him how much he owed his father. No way could he up and leave him... But damn, getting the fuck out of here was one hell of a dream.

He stumbled to the door, eyeing Nikki through the crack

as he unlatched the chain. Her eyes swept up his body, arousal tinging the air. Woman was in permanent heat, though given her age, that wasn't surprising. Around thirty female shifters got desperate to breed, but Jesus, he didn't want that stank in his room. He blocked her entry.

"I'm sorry, okay?" She glanced away as a door opened and shut farther down the hall. "Do we have to do this out here?"

"Yeah."

She huffed her bangs from her eyes. Her brow furrowed, walking her fingers up his abs to the ink below his right pec and tracing the line of script. "When'd you get this one?"

—growling—

"Don't fucking touch me. If you've got something to say, say it."

Her hand fell. "Look, you're right. I was out of line down there. Disrespected you. Made you lose face in front of the club. I was just... it's different for the women here. Harder."

—bullshit—

"Might be easier if you minded your place and stop pissing the ol' ladies off."

The rage that flashed over her face proved his cat right. This was damage control, her trying to manipulate his emotions and suck him back into her lies. He snorted, and she blinked at him, crocodile innocent again.

"We had a deal, Nikki. But all the shit you've been pulling is making that null and void. I'm not the only one with a past. I gave you my word, but keep it up, and I'll have nothing to lose handing your ass over to Hellspawn."

Her eyes narrowed at the mention of the MC down south she'd run riot through before landing here. "You wouldn't."

"Keep pushing and find out."

Nikki's mouth soured, aging her a good ten years. A new name and extreme makeover didn't change the fact that she had a bounty on her head. They caught wind she was here, and they'd be across the country faster than she could blink, hot for blood.

"Fine," she spat out. His eyebrow cocked, and she sighed, chewing her lip. "But we need to sell this, Grim. The table will object to you making me your queen. No one believes we're together… let me stay with you tonight."

—NO—

Grim crossed his arms, leaning against the jamb. "So after that shit downstairs, I'm just supposed to take you back? How the fuck does that look?"

She shrugged, twisting her fingers together. "If you bit me—"

"Not happening." He went to slam the door in her face.

"Wait!" She jammed a leg through the crack, pushing into his room. "It doesn't have to mean—"

"Yeah, it does." He jabbed a finger at her. "You're not my fucking mate."

"You make me your queen, I might as well be," she shot back.

Grim laughed. "Get out."

She closed the door and sauntered over to his recliner, plopping down on the edge of the seat. "No."

Motherf—He pinched the bridge of his nose, then ripped away the afghan she was wrapping around herself. "Don't fucking touch that."

"But I'll get cold."

He eyed the torn teddy she was still wearing. "Not my fucking problem."

"You really are a dick."

"And you're stinking up my room. Close your damned legs."

She arched an eyebrow, sitting back, and looked around, unimpressed. Granted, it was one of the smallest rooms in the club. Ratty recliner, dresser. Bed and a nightstand. Door to the right went to a tiny bathroom. One to the left was a half-empty closet. But to him, it was a fucking palace. Clay had tried to give him a bigger suite and the panic attacks had been intense.

Nothing good happened in big bedrooms.

"Can I take one of those?" Nikki pointed a manicured finger at the rucked-up pile of blankets in the corner his cat used.

—growling—

"You wanna ask Darke?"

Her throat bobbed, and she drew her knees up to her chest.

[SMUG]

Grim flopped back onto the bed, snagging his headphones again. He rolled away from Nikki and got comfortable, pulling the afghan to his nose. His tension faded as he inhaled its elusive scent. It was the one Clay had wrapped around his cat when he'd taken them from Reaper. Something about it... mmph. Just made him feel better, even with his back to the devil. His eyelids drooped, exhaustion hitting him hard. *Looks like you got third shift, buddy. Watch her ass.*

—grumbling—

Suck it up... And he was out.

CHAPTER TWO

GRIM WOKE UP to a hand wrapped around his hard cock.

"Damn, Grimmers, you're fucking huge…" a voice purred in his ear, stroking it. Her leg moved to straddle him.

He bolted out of bed, panting in the early morning light. "The fuck, Nikki!"

She pouted in the nest of blankets he'd left, watching his dick go flaccid.

You were supposed to be watching her ass!

—sorry—

He threw the door open. "Get out."

"I don't understand—"

"No shit. Leave."

Her lips flattened, and she stormed past him in a cloud of mating pheromones. Grim slammed his door shut and threw the chain, then jacked open the window. Fucking room stank like her cunt. Shower didn't do much to improve his mood. He threw on some clothes, snagging a cut from his closet—

Somebody knocked on the door.

"What?" He growled, shoving his arms through the vest.

"It's me."

Shit. Triss. Grim ran a hand over his face and let her in. She scrunched up her nose, pigtails bouncing as she recoiled.

"Ew, gross. No wonder you're in a bad mood. Nikki left a

few minutes ago, if it makes you feel any better. Sorry she didn't take her stank with her."

It should, but somehow didn't. Triss patted the med kit looped over her shoulder. "Doc wants me to check your stitches before table meets, so hurry up and strip."

Grim complied, wincing.

"Ohh… this looks like shit," she said, cheerfully ripping off the bandage.

He rolled his eyes. Girl was like a Pollyanna / Harley Quinn mashup. She pulled out the antiseptic and started swabbing.

"Why doesn't that shit burn like the stuff Doc uses?"

Triss giggled. "Because she thinks the more it hurts, the less likely you guys are to get yourselves banged up in the first place. These should go back in…" She dabbed around a section of popped stitches and glanced at him askance. "But I know you're just gonna pop 'em again. Lucky for you, I've got laceration closures and a shit ton of glue."

"Why didn't she do that in the first place?"

"Samsies as the ethyl alcohol. And if you didn't fuck them up, the stitches would heal cleaner." She glanced at him around her tube of glue. That fucking stung. Triss pinched the sides of his wound together, uncharacteristically serious. "You wanna talk about it?"

"No." But if he had, Triss would've been his first choice. Girl was like the little sister he never wanted. He forced a smile. "I'm fine."

"Lies," she sang, tossing the glue back into her bag and pulling out a laceration kit. "But it's okay, I'm not up for any girly sharing time this morning either."

Grim cocked an eyebrow. Since when? Triss was usually a rolling stream of consciousness.

She sighed and then her face screwed up like an evil pixie's. "I was here last night. Doc didn't want me at the vet's alone after you guys got hit… Deuce saw me, Grim. And for two seconds I thought—" She shook her head, tearing into the package. "Stupid jerk pushed right past me and had that molly suck his dick. And I was all like, fine, whatever about it, right?"

"Right."

"Wrong." She affixed some funky looking wing things around his wound. "Soon as I started talking to Riff, Deuce comes over, scares him off, then sits there, totally ignoring me. Like, what the fuck!"

"I dunno."

"And we're back to lies." Triss frowned, pulling the wings tight across the wound and sticking them down. Shit was slick and felt a hell of a lot better than the stitches had. "He's your bestie. You'd tell me if I had even an eensy chance, wouldn't you?"

Grim scratched the back of his neck. "It's complicated."

"Ooooh!" She perked up, clasping her hands under her chin.

He groaned, not wanting to give her false hope. Deuce was stubborn as fuck. "That doesn't mean—"

"Yup, it does. And you know at some point you're gonna have to spill. About him and Nikki." She taped a pad of gauze over her work. "You two are not currently cultivating a healthy relationship."

Grim snorted, easing back into his T. Understatement of the century, there.

"Need me to wash your sheets?" Triss asked, sniffing again as she packed up her kit.

"Nah, I'll get one of the ol' ladies to—"

"Wouldn't bet on that," she said, throwing her bag over her shoulder. "Hanna's pissed about you fucking Nikki on the bar after she said something."

"I didn't fuck her."

Triss rolled her eyes. "Okay, after you finger banged her on the bar."

He scratched his jaw. Right. That he did do. "I was gonna clean it after table meets."

"Too late. She's already sanitized it, twice." She tapped her lip and shrugged. "Maybe more. I'd torch it and get a new one, but that's just me. How about I take care of your sheets and you give me a ride back to the vet's later?"

"Might be awhile, I was gonna do some work on the bike."

"Works for me." She grinned. "That'll give me time for Operation Deuce."

Operation—nope. Didn't want to know. Grim shrugged into his cut and stood. "Thanks for taking care of my shoulder."

Triss waved it away and blew him a kiss, already gone.

He stripped the bed and followed, pausing to reset the code locking the door. This one he wouldn't be sharing with Mouse.

Grim strode through the clubhouse, enjoying the quiet of the early hour. He dropped his laundry by the machine, no idea how that shit worked. Clanking and laughter came from the kitchen. It cut off when he stepped over the threshold to grab a coffee, an icy silence in its place. Triss raised an eyebrow at him from the other end of the long prep table. Shit. She hadn't been kidding.

"Mornin' Hanna," he said, grabbing a pot of coffee and a mug.

Woman glared at him, smacking down a spatula. The rest of the ol' ladies in the kitchen did this synchronized arm crossing routine behind her. "Don't you mornin' me, Grimdarke James."

"Look. I'm sorry about last night. I was gonna scrub the bar down after table meets, but Triss said you beat me to it. It won't happen again."

"See that it don't," she sniffed, not mollified in the slightest. "Can't say I'm upset about you taking issue with what

that whore molly's been up to, though. She needs to go."
Murmurs of agreement came from the other ol' ladies.

"Caught the bitch rubbin' up on my ol' man," one of them
said. "She wants to burn through brothers, fine, but lifting tail
around our claimed mates? Fuck that shit. Ain't how it works,
and I don't give a fuck if she is MK's daughter. Girl should
know better."

Grim grunted his agreement, leaning back against the
counter. "I spoke with her last night."

"That what you're callin' it?" Another snickered.

"Hush," Hanna chided. "I believe it way she tore out of
here this morning."

"She say where she was going?"

They all looked at him like he was stupid.

"Cat House," Triss said, naming the MC-owned strip club.
"Tonight's brother's choice."

"She's probably headed there early to slick the soles of the
competition's stilettos," Hanna added. The ol' ladies snickered, going back to prepping breakfast.

"All the mollys will be there trying to win the pot," Triss
said. "Think it's up to a grand."

"Two grand," Deuce said, coming in and grabbing a mug.
"My money's on Kelsey." He waggled his eyebrows at Grim.
"She used to be a gymnast."

"Psh," Trish buzzed her lips. "That's only because you
haven't seen my routine yet."

The coffee pot smashed down on the counter and Deuce
swore, jerking back from the deluge of hot brew.

Hanna rushed over with a towel. "You cut yourself?"

"Nah," he glowered at Triss from the corner of his eye and
waved his bandaged hand. "Just lost my grip. Sorry about
that."

"Mmm…" Hanna hummed with a funny smile, cleaning
up the mess.

"You got your outfit?" One of the ol' ladies asked Triss.

"Oh my God, yes! I'll have to show you, it's like this total peek-a-boo, totally sheer cheerleading thingy."

Deuce started coughing.

"You okay, buddy?" Grim asked, smacking him on the back.

"Fucking peachy."

"And I'm bringing my mini-trampoline," Triss squealed.

Deuce made a pained grunt.

"Come on, we're gonna be late to table." Grim snickered, earning himself a scowl as they exited the kitchen. "Dude, if you just—" He raised his hands at the look his friend shot him. "Fine. But you know, she's gonna hook up with someone—"

"Over my dead body." Deuce growled, pushing into the office and taking his seat at the long table the club officers met at. He snatched his pen and pad, looking like he wanted to take heads as opposed to minutes.

Grim pulled out his chair at Clay's right hand. Worry and exhaustion lined his father's face. The last three weeks had been hard on him.

Stitch, Triss's father and the club's sergeant at arms, sat to his left with a similar expression. Beside him was MK's empty chair, then Brick, their enforcer, and Miser, the club treasurer. Mouse was set up at the far end with his laptop, and Deacon, their chaplain, sat between him and Grim.

Clay smacked down his gavel and called the meeting to order.

"First up, that shit show last night." He sighed. "Cantone's fucking rabid. He's got Ottawa locked down and isn't letting anyone piss over the border until he sorts his people out. That gang banger Grim brought back spilled a name, but Mouse hasn't been able to get a hit on it."

"Oh, I got plenty of hits," the tech nerd muttered, pushing his thick glasses up the bridge of his nose. "That's the problem. Caleb Judah has got more identities associated with him than Brick has outstanding warrants for assault after Rendezvous."

Grim's stomach dropped as Mouse shot the big man a pointed look.

Brick shrugged. "People shouldn't cut in line."

"Anyway," Mouse continued, "sorting through them's on par with tracking down all the social media feeds of him beating the shit out of those guys."

"You don't have to," Grim breathed out. "It was Reaper."

Every eye at the table landed on him.

Mouse blinked like an owl. "Not possible. Prick's still in jail."

"For three more years after putting a bullet in my ol' lady's head," Clay growled.

"Look, all I know is that's one of his aliases," Grim muttered, chewing on his lip. "Caleb, from the tribe of Judah, was one of the twelve spies Moses sent into Canaan."

Brick snorted. "That some fucked up Bible shit? Didn't know you were so pious, Grim."

Beside him, Deacon snorted. Dude was a dick.

"I'm not, but Reaper is... well, more like a fanatic." And he'd beaten the gospel into Grim at an early age. "There a Seth Asher or a Sham Reuben on your list, Mouse?"

"Sec... I'm cross referencing—Damn. Yeah, variations of all of them pop up..."

"Lemme see?"

Mouse slid the laptop down the table, and Grim skimmed the spreadsheet—

Shit.

He pushed the laptop back to Mouse. "He wants us to know it's him."

"Care to explain your rationale?" Stitch asked, clicking on his vape. Out of all the original founders, he was the one most willing to give Grim a fair shake.

Not that he wanted one at the moment. Grim scrubbed at

his face, wishing he'd kept his damned mouth shut. "There's another name on there, Matthias Stone. That was the alias he used for me last time we crossed the border."

The table was silent for half a beat.

"Any relation to the Matthias Stone flagged as a person of interest in multiple grisly murders outside of Toronto?" Mouse asked, his fingers flying over the keyboard.

"Feds pulled us in for questioning about that," Deacon snarled.

Yep. Should have kept his mouth shut.

Mouse turned his laptop to flash the table Grim's juvie mug-shot. "Aww. You were a cute little ax murder... and delete..."

"Didn't use an ax," he muttered.

Mouse's brow rose. "Bayonet? Meat cleaver?"

"Machete."

"Nice."

Stitch cleared his throat. "If Reaper's influence has expanded this much while he's still in prison, we've got a real problem. Only reason we've got half the contracts we do is because Satan's Vengeance is a bunch of monkeys without him at the helm. PD's constantly picking the idiots up."

"And those contracts have taken a serious hit over the past six months," Miser added, all sour. Man was as cuddly as his name suggested. "Our profits are down forty-seven percent. Only steady earners are the brick-and-mortar businesses in town, and that'll be steadily nothing as soon as the snow flies and the tourists piss off."

"Is Reaper using the prison's internet to get messages out?" Clay asked.

Mouse snorted. "I would've caught it. I've got that shit locked down tight, and they scan all the physical mail... I mean, I doubt he's got someone on the inside with the amount we're shelling out... and the man's in solitary.

Records say he got into it with a couple guards three weeks ago. Added six months on to his sentence."

"And no visitors per his sentencing," Stitch mused.

"Regardless, I'm in agreement with Grim." Clay frowned. "Reaper might be batshit crazy, but he's card-carrying Mensa material. Somehow, he's in contact with his crew."

Brick cracked his knuckles. "Then we take out SV."

"To what end?" Clay asked. "None of their members have been directly involved with any of this shit. We move on them, we just add to the list of people actively gunning for us. I need to know how he's passing info and to who." He turned to Mouse. "Double whatever you've got running at the prison. Reaper farts, I wanna know how wet it is."

"All ready on it."

Clay grunted. "Back to Cantone. With Ottawa locked down for the foreseeable future, we got no buyer, and the cartel is looking to get paid. How bad is that gonna burn us?"

Miser grimaced. "It won't put us in the red, but it's fucking close."

"That's what I thought." Clay chewed his lip. "Russians reached out a while back, but they broker through the witches. I ain't keen on getting into bed with either." There was a general murmur of agreement around the table. "I'm also not sure we have a choice. That visit from Sheriff Dales this morning was enlightening on a number of fronts. Come the first of the month, the Feds is setting up a field office in Rensselaer Falls."

Grim frowned. Wasn't exactly the kind of place an operation like that would pick unless they had a damned good reason, and he was pretty sure the lovely college campuses weren't it.

"Needless to say, holding on to merchandise strikes me as a bad idea. Let's put it to a vote. All in favor of dealing with the witches?"

Three hands went up. Grim's wasn't one of them.

"All in favor of waiting for Cantone to clean house?"

Grim and Stitch raised their hands. Clay snorted, shaking his head. "And were he here, MK's vote would make that a tie. What about you, Mouse?"

"Hmm? Me? I didn't know I had a vote."

"You don't, I'm just curious."

The wiry man pushed up his glasses again. "Both carry equal risk, but I'd rather deal with the Paranormal Council than the Feds if things go bad."

"Good point," Clay murmured, then smacked the table with his gavel. "Fuck it. Witches it is. I'll set it up, and going forward, we're making straight runs. Same day pick up and drop. I'm tired of cleaning body parts off my mountain—and speaking of body parts," he turned to Deacon, "with the Feds setting up shop, none of the mollys at the Cat House lift their tails until further notice. Our businesses need to be above reproach, especially that one. Feds'll spin it into a prostitution ring quicker than you can blink."

The chaplain's bloodless lips soured, but he nodded. "I'll handle it."

"Miser—"

"Books are already cooked."

Clay snorted. "Figured as much. I was gonna ask how Hanna is. Hear tell there's some friction between the ol' ladies and the mollys."

The older man ran a hand through his thinning salt and pepper hair, glancing at Grim. "She ain't happy. Mollys've been breaking rank, trying to cozy up to mated brothers, pushing back on what they can and can't do. Found two of them in my office painting their damned nails the other day."

"Didn't realize it'd gotten so bad... I've been distracted of late." Clay pursed his lips. "And I'll own up to the fact that part of that's my fault for not taking a mate. Tell Hanna I appreciate her stepping up and doin' what she can to fill the role for the club." Miser grunted his thanks, and Clay swiveled in his seat to look at Grim.

"However, that shit's gotta stop. Women'll make or break a club. They might not know everything, but they see enough, and all it takes is one of them club-sluts flapping their lips to the wrong person. Since MK's not here and surer than shit, Nikki's instigating all this, you're gonna take point."

Grim winced. "I talked to her last night—"

"Talk to her again. MK's one of my best friends, and a founder of this club, but enough allowances have been made for his brat. If she doesn't tone it the fuck down, she's gone. I won't have division in my house. We clear?"

"Crystal." Grim scratched his jaw, trying not to smile. Clay's version of gone was six feet under and would be Christmas come early.

[JOY JOY JOY]

"Good," his father said, settling back in his chair. "Anything else we need to discuss? No? Then get out. Grim, you stay."

Shit. Deuce shot him a sympathetic look as he pushed in his chair and the rest of the table left the room. Clay stared at Grim, their features too similar for anyone not to know they were blood with a glance.

"What are you thinking, son?"

Well, that was a loaded question. He met Clay's grey-blue eyes, the concern in them a punch in the gut. "About what?"

"Reaper left those breadcrumbs for you."

He wasn't wrong, but Grim didn't want to talk about it. He picked at the table's veneer. "You would've figured it out."

"Doubtful. I'm not exactly well versed in Biblical Israeli spies."

The silence stretched between them, palpable.

"It's a game to him," Grim finally said. "He's leading us around by the nose, dropping bombs to see how we react."

"Like a test?"

"No… I dunno, maybe… when your prey's reacting, they can't respond. He's keeping us busy, so we don't notice what else he's doing. The fact that the distraction's causing damage is just gravy, and him using those aliases… It's a fucking allegory. I guarantee he's got eleven more irons in the fire to stab us with."

Clay pursed his lips. "So why put your alias in there?"

"You think I'm one of the spies?"

"No. If it's a game, I think he sees you as his opponent."

Grim snorted. "Trust me, he's made it very fucking clear that out of the three of us, Shiv got the brains and Grapple got the brawn. I was just the shit that was leftover."

"You really believe that?"

Grim stood, slamming his chair against the table. "Yeah, I do. We done here?"

Clay sighed. "For now. And son?"

Grim's hand froze on the door's handle.

"I've known Reaper a long time. Man has a habit of undermining the confidence of anyone he feels is a threat. If he made such a point of cutting you down, maybe it's time you start wondering why."

"I'll add it to my list," Grim muttered, leaving his father at the table.

He made his way through the clubhouse, brain on overload with shit he didn't want to think about. Fucking Reaper. Clay was right about one thing, that alias of Grim's had been planted to get a reaction out of him. But what the fuck was Reaper hoping to achieve, letting them know he was behind the issues with their runs?

Grim pushed through the front door, scuffing his boots through the gravel lot. Casting doubt over his loyalty to the MC was the easy answer. Deuce, Brick, and Mouse knew it was horseshit, probably Stitch… but the rest of the table? They'd voted against him getting patched in as VP.

Didn't trust him after eighteen years with Reaper. Shit. He wouldn't either.

Grim scratched his jaw, squinting up at the sun. There had to be more to it. He shook his head and started pushing his bike to the garage.

According to the Bible, Caleb had been one of two spies sent to explore Canaan that'd come back and declared it conquerable. The other ten spies disagreed. God disagreed with their disagreement and eighty-sixed them. Since the rest of the Israelites had agreed with the ten, they got to wander around in the desert for forty years—one for every day the spies had scouted Canaan.

Grim frowned, kicking down the bike's stand and going to grab tools. How long had Reaper been in jail? There was probably some fucked up correlation. Though, considering the man was crazier than a shithouse rat, it could be the fucking days between his bowel movements.

Whatever. Trying to figure out Reaper's logic was pointless. What Grim needed to be focused on was taking his bike apart to get at the carb.

"Need some help?" Triss bounced into the garage on the toes of her boots, grinning.

Grim sat back on his haunches. "Are you really gonna dance tonight?"

"Did you see Deuce's face?" She laughed, clapping her hands.

"Yeah, I did, and that's not an answer."

"Psh." She rolled her eyes. "My parents would kill me… but that doesn't mean I can't show up in costume…" She twirled around giggling, her trapeze shirt flying up and showing an uncomfortable amount of barely legal flesh.

Grim looked away. "Save it for the strip club."

"Are you gonna be there?"

"Who else is gonna help Deuce bury the bodies of your suitors?"

"Yay!" Triss clapped her hands. "Want me to get that? Little fingers," she said, waggling them.

"Go for it."

Between the two of them, they got the carb off and apart in record time. Shit pissed fuel all over his boots when Triss fucked with the drain screw before he was ready, but whatever. Bored with helping, she brought them lunch, then sat on the workbench, dangling her feet and watching him remove the old jets.

"How'd you learn to do all that?"

He shrugged. "Pretty much by what you're doing now. Hanging around and annoying the fuck out of guys who knew what they were doing."

Triss laughed. "Glad I can be of service."

Grim wiped his forehead against his arm, wincing as his stitches pulled. "You see Nikki when you were grabbing lunch?"

"Nope. One of the mollys was bitching about her though. It's not just the mated brothers she's messing with, whenever one of them grabs a brother's interest, Nikki makes sure it doesn't last... you think she's been with Deuce?"

"I dunno. He hasn't said anything, but I'd be surprised."

"Bro code?"

"Something like that."

"Why her, Grim? You could have any of them. I mean, she's pretty and all, but you can do so much better."

He laughed. "Yeah, like who?"

"I dunno." She shrugged. "Maybe you haven't met her yet."

"Maybe she doesn't exist."

"Doubtful." Triss rolled her eyes. "Everyone has one true mate."

"And you think yours is Deuce?"

"My cat does," she murmured. "I don't know what I think."

Grim wiped his hand on a rag and grabbed one of the needle jets, spraying it down with carburetor cleaner before dropping it in and cinching it down. "In my experience, most of the time my cat's full of shit."

—hey!—

Truth.

"Mmm." Triss chewed on her fingernail. "Mine just wants what she wants."

"Yeah, that too. Pass me that wrench."

She handed it over. "Are you gonna let Nikki know you're going tonight?"

Grim glanced at his phone. It'd been suspiciously silent all day. Usually she was blowing it up with selfies and other stupid shit. The absence made him nervous as hell. "No."

Triss raised an eyebrow, and he busied himself putting his carburetor back together. Granted, going to the Cat House wasn't something he did often—seemed kind of pointless to get all hot and bothered over women he had zero chance of fucking—but it wasn't like he'd never been.

"Oooh, wait—so you're like, what, checking up on her after last night?"

"Sure. If you want to call it that." It was more like having Deuce's back, but whatever. Triss being there was gonna make him nuts. And after Grim delivered Clay's ultimatum to Nikki? He didn't give a damn what she did. Hopefully, she'd fuck up royal and put everyone out of their misery when she got "gone."

Triss buzzed her lips. "What are you doing now?"

"Shimming the needle."

"English, please."

Grim snorted, glancing at her askance. "Making an adjustment so the fuel mixture's richer. Should stop the bike from backfiring."

"Right, that still made no sense except for the last part,

and I'm sad. That's like, your calling card. Ba Boom! Oh, Grim's here!"

"Great," he muttered, re-seating the diaphragm. Now his bike was a damned joke, too.

Triss seemed to sense his mood, because she was quiet for the rest of the afternoon, handing him tools without comment. He assembled the last of it, and threw a leg over.

"Well, you ready?"

A smile bloomed across her face. "Really?"

"Yeah, you think I was gonna take you back to the vet's in a cage? Grab those domes and let's test her out."

She squealed and thrust one of the helmets at him, tightening her own and hopping on. Bike started like a fucking dream, and he revved it, then let it drop back to idle. Nice. Grim glanced at her over his shoulder, and Triss's arms wrapped around his waist.

They took off, out of the compound.

Sun was still brilliant, a handsbreadth above the horizon. The late summer greenery fluttered in their wake as they tore down the backroads, a cloud of dust behind them.

"Woo! Go faster!" Triss screamed in his ear.

How could he say no, and fuck if his Bobber didn't perform. They pulled into the decrepit strip mall at the edge of town way too soon.

Triss hopped off, grinning ear to ear. "Woot! That was awesome!"

"Thanks for helping. You need a ride tonight?"

She shook her head. "I'm getting ready at a friend's house, and we're going together."

"See you there, then."

She kissed his cheek and skipped into the vet's. Grim waited until her pigtails disappeared through the inside door leading down to the underground infirmary before heading back to the club.

He took the ride home slower, the throbbing in his

shoulder more noticeable without Triss egging him on. As unbelievable as it was, he missed her stream of consciousness. Without it, his mind drifted right back to Reaper.

That asshole had been the one that'd taught Grim how to clean a carb and do just about everything else with a bike. Yeah, the man was a fucking psycho ninety percent of the time, but the ten percent he wasn't... that's what fucked with Grim. Those few and far in-between times when he acted like he cared... almost like a dad.

Those were times Grim held onto when he was getting the shit beaten out of him for his latest infraction. Why he'd tried so hard to win the bastard's approval. Clay wasn't like that. He just *gave,* and Grim still couldn't understand why. He hadn't earned any of it.

—loves us—

Grim snorted. Leaving him with Reaper for the better part of his life said otherwise, and neither him nor his cat were worthy of it. At least not yet.

Maybe never.

[SHAME]

He pulled into the clubhouse lot and killed his engine. Retreated to his room like a thief in the night, the joy of his bike not backfiring sullied.

CHAPTER THREE

FLATTS WAS the typical tourist town. Pretty little mom and pop shops selling tchotchkes standing along a tree-lined Main Street. Cafe on the corner that served decent coffee and killer cinnamon rolls. Some chichi French nouveau whatever mid-strip that would be gone by spring. Tattoo parlor the club owned was tucked between the antiques dealer and the local art gallery.

Not quite a third of the big windows were shuttered, which wasn't too bad, considering the economy was shit. Grim rode past them all, avoiding the orange safety cone marking the pothole the town had been promising to fix for the last eight weeks after some blonde had hit it and broke her axle.

Wrench had been bitching about it ever since. He'd ended up working on her car when it landed at the club's garage a couple streets down. Business was steady, if not good, but that's what happens when you were the only mechanic for miles.

Same deal with the strip club on the opposite edge of town. The Cat House was in the defunct rail yard, in part of the old roundhouse they'd used for the servicing and storing the locomotives way back when.

Grim thumped over the tracks, later than he'd wanted to be. Bikes and cages already filled the main lot. He rode around to the side yard. It would be a walk, but better than some drunken asshole plowing into his ride.

Music and the sounds of people partying filtered through the night. He hooked the strap of his dome over the handlebars and started walking. At least the weather was nice. He passed a couple fucking in the back of a pickup at the edge of the lot, and another group toking up. No one from the MC yet, but they were probably all inside—

"You think Grim's coming tonight?"

His steps slowed, not recognizing the nasally voice coming from around the corner. Sounded young, early twenties, maybe.

"Doubtful. He never fucking shows. Man, if I had a piece of ass like Nikki, I wouldn't let her out of my sight."

That one he did recognize. It was one of the new prospects they'd picked up… Derek? Devon? Whatever it was, dipshit had a stupid accent. Kid's parents ran that French place doomed to fail on Main.

"You fuck her yet?"

Well, this just got interesting. Grim stopped, falling back into the shadows to listen.

"Not yet, but I'm gonna. She let me suck her tits."

—growling—

Grim frowned, in agreement with his cat. They didn't take prospects until they were eighteen, but Jesus fuck, Nikki was thirty-two. He scratched his jaw, realizing there was also about fourteen years between Deuce and Triss. Granted, she was twenty-one, but still…

Huh. Maybe Deuce had a point.

"So what do we do if Grim comes?"

"You'll hear his bike backfire. If you do, just go inside and tell Deacon. He'll take care of the rest."

Grim's eyebrow rose. Was that fucking right? Not that he was totally surprised, man wasn't exactly his bestie… but Grim was his VP whether he liked it or not.

He needed to find out what Deacon was hiding.

Wasn't gonna happen going in the front door, though. Grim backtracked to the cordoned-off portion of the round-house. Shit was sealed up tighter than he remembered, but then, the last time he'd slunk through these shadows, he'd been younger than those dipshits at the door.

He cast an eye around the lot, subtly shifting the musculature of his legs—

And jumping onto the roof.

—nice—

Desperate times. There wasn't a fucking ladder.

Grim crept close to the eaves, dim light coming from the massive soffit vents. Weird. This part of the roundhouse should be abandoned. He pulled his knife, working the edge of one until it came loose. He slowly pried it free and moved it to the side.

A dozen-ish reworked train cars filled the space. The closest was about a five-foot drop below him. Christmas lights had been strung up around wooden walkways connecting them like spokes on a wheel. Shades were only partially drawn on one of the far cars, and through the gap a large red-haired man was sucking off another guy in flannel.

The fuck?

A door opened, and a woman with a lantern in her hand laughed, leading another man to a different car. Grim frowned. The Cat house definitely wasn't a straight-up strip club, but he was under the impression the girls gave extra favors in the private booths, and dudes had never been part of the equation. This shit was next level. Did Clay know? His comment about the Feds thinking it was a prostitution ring…

Grim ran a hand over his jaw. He didn't fucking know, and that bothered him. As VP, he should have a handle on all of the club's business, not just dealing arms. But given what Clay knew about Grim's past, would he have kept this from him? Would Deuce? Wrench? Bastards were here all the time.

What else didn't he know about?

[ANGER]

Yeah. Lots of that. Grim shimmied the vent enough to lower himself onto the roof of the car below and jumped down, keeping to the shadows. Large support beams holding up the roof caged in the cars, the rest of the space was barren. He peeked into a car's window. This one was empty, tricked out with pillows and scarves like a harem. The next was some kind of a sex dungeon, a St. Andrew's Cross at the far end with whips and floggers lining the wall.

He made his way around the perimeter, stomach sinking. The few cars he peered into each had a theme, and more than half of them were filled with customers. Shit had to be raking in a mint; no way was the profit on Deacon's books legit.

The door the woman had led her john through before opened again, the faint pounding of bass slipping through. Grim ducked behind a support beam. Another whore sauntered into the room with a lantern and man in tow. The hallway they'd come down was pitch black. As soon as they'd disappeared into one of the cars, Grim made for the door, his vision subtly shifting as darkness enveloped him. Colors bled out and the flat planes of the walls sharpened.

The hall was narrow and took a circuitous route, not part of the original structure. Pin points of light at eye level shot through the darkness; viewing holes into various rooms of the club. He tried to orient himself, the one in front of him peering into the dancer's dressing room.

"She's such a fucking bitch," a blonde wearing wings seethed, brushing her hair at a cheap vanity. She was the molly from the club that'd been sucking off Deuce last night.

"Careful, she's probably listening..." a woman out of sight said.

"I don't give a fuck, Grim seems like a genuinely good guy and all she does is piss all over him the way she spreads her legs for anything with a dick."

"Pretty sure it doesn't need a dick way she was munching carpet earlier on stage." The other woman laughed. "And I dunno. I mean, granted, the man is built like a God, but a good guy? More like dumb as fuck the way he lets her run around on him."

"He's VP, he can't be that dumb."

"You ever hear him string more than two sentences together?"

"Well, no, but he doesn't exactly party like the rest of them —Whatever. I wouldn't run around on him even if he was. Why does Nikki need our men drooling after her, too?"

A brunette strutted over, taking the brush from her. "Because she's a self-centered cunt, but once he makes her his queen, she'll forget about the rest of them."

The blonde sniffled. "Not fucking likely. God, if Grim ever gave me the time of day—"

"She'd beat the shit out of you, then do something horrible to ruin your life. I told you, she ran one molly off for offering him a napkin, and she already hates you."

"Doesn't matter, he won't, and I'm leaving anyway. I got my acceptance letter…"

Grim stepped back and frowned. Jesus fuck, was that what everyone thought about him? He raked a hand through his hair and moved farther down the hall. It made a sharp bend, abruptly ending somewhere behind the main stage, if he had to guess. The door was made from the roundhouse's original wood and didn't open like a regular door. He fiddled with it for a moment; it sank towards him, then retracted into a pocket, music pulsing louder. A heavy velvet curtain blocked his view of what was on the other side.

The DJ's voice boomed out, announcing the next dancer. The curtain swayed, a shadow passing across the sliver of light below the curtain. Raucous catcalls sounded, but he didn't hear anyone else close.

Grim's fingers found the edge of the curtain, and he slid

out. Yeah, he was backstage, the crowd visible through a break in the backdrop. Place was fucking slammed. He looked around, moving behind a rack of costumes and props left forgotten in the wings.

Mollys worked the crowd in skimpy little bits of nothing, moving to the pounding beat. Smoke hung lank in the air, swirling around the undulations of the stripper on stage. Room was packed with brothers throwing back drinks, and the card tables along the far wall were piled with chips. Wrench sat at one of them with Deuce, the two of them in animated conversation.

Grim followed his friend's pissed off gaze to Triss, sitting at the bar with a group of girls. Goddamn. They'd all decked themselves out like cheerleaders, skirts so short their ass cheeks were hanging out, and their see-through jerseys were looped up between their tits to show off their flat stomachs.

Triss's abs had a big ass two drawn on them. Deuce had to be losing his fucking mind. Christ, Grim had to fight the urge to go out there and cover her up. Some douche in a polo worked his way over to introduce himself, and Triss beamed at him, sucking on a lollypop.

Grim's eyes went back to Deuce. He'd sat back in his chair, sipping on his drink, glare burning a hole in the back of the douche's head. No fucking good was gonna come of that. Grim frowned, scanning the room for Nikki.

His eyes flicked to the upper level. Private parties rented out the balcony with its second bar. A sign that said "Reserved" was clipped onto the velvet rope, but the only person up there was a bartender setting up. An old foreman's office was next to the party room. Deacon had claimed that for his own, the big glass windows looking out over the club floor. Desk lamp was on, but the office was empty.

Grim checked the time on his phone. It was still early for a party, only a little after ten, but where the hell was—

The crowd erupted as the DJ called for a round of

applause, the dancer bending to collect her tips. She waved with a bow and retreated backstage, muttering about her shoes slipping and cheap assholes as she clacked back to the dressing room.

"Who the fuck left this door open?"

The curtain Grim had slunk past whipped open and Deacon came out, his arm wrapped around Nikki's waist. He pulled the door shut behind them and pushed her up against it. "Was it you?"

"No, Daddy," she simpered.

"Mmm. I think I'll punish you anyway." He lowered his mouth to hers and started tongue fucking her as she unbuttoning his pants.

—cum slut—

Yeah. Grim swallowed the bile in his throat, unable to tear his eyes away. Deacon kneed apart her thighs, and she rubbed herself against him shamelessly, hand pumping his wizened cock.

"Those two in the back weren't enough for you?" Deacon breathed, biting at her neck.

"It gets me so hot when you watch…"

He chuckled, shoving his hand between her legs. "You need me to fuck all this cum deeper into your ass, baby?"

She moaned, and he flipped her around, burying his dick between her cheeks.

—growling—

Grim ran a hand down his face. Fuck. He'd known she was a slut, but Jesus Christ. Shit wouldn't matter if she was happy being a molly; it was their fucking job to service the club, but after what'd gone down between them last night…

Shit wasn't gonna change.

Which made no goddamned sense. Nikki was smarter than this. Something else had to be up. If her goal was to be Grim's queen, alpha over the rest of the club females, she'd be keeping her legs together.

He slipped away into the crowd on the main floor, making a beeline for the bar. Triss spotted him over the polo douche's shoulder and waved. Douche shot him a frown, trying to catch her attention again.

Good fucking luck.

She bounced off her seat, her tits doing things Grim really shouldn't be noticing, and caught him up in a big hug. "You made it!"

"Yeah," He mussed his hair. "I'm here, all right."

Her eyes narrowed. "What happened?"

"Just saw Nikki taking it up the ass." Triss's mouth rounded to an 'o' and he laughed. "Yep. And Deacon was the one plowing her."

"Eww." Her nose scrunched up. "He smells like old cheese."

Not an inaccurate descriptor. Grim flagged down the bartender and ordered a bottle. Man took one look at him and didn't offer a glass to go with. Smart.

"So, what are you gonna do?" Triss asked.

Grim tipped the bottle back, throat bobbing. "Not a damned thing."

"What?" Her brow furrowed. "You don't seem real upset."

He shrugged. "She's a molly. It's what they do."

"Yeah… but I thought—"

"So did she. Let's keep it that way for now."

Triss's eyes rolled to the back of her head. "Fine. I won't say anything, but really? Deacon? He's like eighty."

Grim snorted, choking on his mouthful. "More like late sixties, but I didn't think an age gap bothered you."

Cue the eye roll again. "That's not a gap, it's a trench. He has liver spots, Grim. Liv-ver." She glanced past him, and her eyes lit up. A second later, a hand clasped Grim's shoulder.

"Hey man, you made it! Who we talking about?"

"Hi Deuce," Triss drawled, swishing her skirt around her hips.

"Hey." He coughed, looking, but trying like hell not to. "Wrench is setting up another hand, you in?"

Grim glanced between them. "If Triss wants to play." No way was he leaving her here with the douche.

She clapped, bouncing on her toes, and Deuce went pale, eyes glued to her tits. She must've noticed, her nipples hardening beneath his heated gaze.

Deuce licked his lips. "I... uh, dunno if that's a good idea..." He shook himself like a dog. "I mean, the buy-in's pretty high."

"How about if I just watch? I can sit with you, right?"

"Um..."

" 'Course you can," Grim said, ignoring the death rays shooting from Deuce's eyes.

They pushed through the crowd to the table.

Wrench looked up from the deck, frowning as Deuce plunked down next to him. "Shit, sorry, Triss, I only saved two chairs—"

"That's fine, I'm just watching." She sat on Deuce's lap before he could protest, one arm around his shoulders. "And you don't mind sharing a seat, do you? I mean, if you'd rather, I'll go hang with Jacob—"

Fire ignited in Deuce's eyes. "Who?"

She pointed at the polo douche eye-fucking her from his seat at the bar. "You know he used to be on a cheer squad? He was telling me about this lift where the girl does a split, and he raises them up over his head..." She shook hers. "I can't quite envision it, so he was gonna show me."

Deuce's fingers caged her hip. "Stay."

"Yay!" She rubbed her hands together, wiggling on his thigh. "Deal us in!"

Grim chuckled, topping off his friend's drink from the bottle. Deuce looked like he was gonna need it. Shit, so did he. The buy-in was high, and Grim played like shit. Well, not a shitty as Deuce, but Triss wasn't exactly making it easy for the poor guy. Way she was squirming all over his lap, no way was his head in the game.

Grim was too busy thinking about Nikki. Why risk their deal to fuck the MC's chaplain? The highest thing most mollys aspired to was pinning down a brother to make them an ol' lady. A queen was a step above, usually reserved for true mates, where the power was shared between them equally. Nikki sure as fuck wasn't his mate, but he'd agreed to make her his queen, and with Grim as VP—maybe someday Prez—she'd be the most influential shifter female in St. Lawrence County by association. What the fuck else could she want?

And more importantly, how did fucking Deacon get her closer to it?

One of the randos at the table tossed more chips into the pot, and Grim folded, sitting back with his bottle. Two things he knew for certain. Just because Clay laid down the law, didn't mean she was gonna follow it, and his father would need hard proof before he followed through with his edict.

Grim needed to stop reacting and do something to make one or the other happen.

"Deep thought over there, brother," Wrench said, matching the bet. On the far side of the room, Nikki came out from the employee's area, surveying the room like she owned it.

"You guys ever fuck one of the whores here?" Grim asked.

Deuce and Wrench exchanged a glance. Triss just narrowed her eyes at him.

"No." Wrench pulled a card from the deck. "Whores ain't my thing."

Deuce snorted. "Yeah, he's more into dumb blondes that drive into potholes."

"Shut the fuck up. Allie's not dumb, she was distracted."

"You must be too, considering how long that axle's taking to replace."

"It's more than the axle, and it's a vintage Bug." Wrench tossed another chip into the pot. "Getting parts is a bitch."

"Dude, there's a VW plant in Ohio, Tennessee—"

"Vin-tage." Wench drawled at Deuce. "Shit's all special order, and takes forever to find. Torsion arm should be in next Saturday—"

"Have you ever fucked a whore here?" Triss asked, turning in Deuce's lap to look at him.

His jaw dropped. "I… uh…"

"That's a yes." Grim laughed, grinning at his friend's glare.

"Fine, it's a yes, but not since I was a prospect," he grumbled. "There's plenty of willing pussy at the club. Why the fuck would I pay for it?"

Grim shrugged, eyeing the curtained off booths lining the far wall, nothing between them and the crowd.

"You thinking about gettin' some strange?" Wrench asked, eyebrow raised.

"Would that be weird?"

His friends looked at each other again, sharing a WTF moment, then spoke at the same time.

"Um… yes. You're like a priest or some shit."

"Dude, I'm not even sure you're fucking Nikki."

"I'd say I'm due then." He nodded to the table next to them. The blonde with wings he'd seen in the dressing room was delivering drinks. "That's Kelsey, right? The gymnast?"

"Indeed, it is," Deuce said, abruptly all business. "And a very good choice. Hey, Kels!"

She looked around at her name, her green eyes wide. Deuce flagged her down, and she smiled, sauntering over. "Hey baby," she gave him a peck on the cheek, then pulled back, running her eyes over Triss. "You two lookin' to party?"

Deuce went scarlet. "I—No. She's not, we're not—"

"You're cute, but I'm all about the D." Triss laughed.

Deuce looked like he was gonna die. "He called you over for Grim."

"Grim?" Kelsey's hand went to her throat.

"Yeah, Grim." His eyes ran over her. She was in stilettos and a purple thong, with star pasties over her nipples. Her bleached hair hung long and poker straight. No wonder Nikki was such a bitch to her. Kelsey was the hot as hell, all-natural version of what Nikki had been going for. He jerked his thumb at the curtained booths. "Feel like giving me a private dance?"

The molly's eyes widened.

So did the rest of the table's.

"Holy shit," Deuce laughed. "Are you really gonna do it?"

—?!—

Play along, asshole. "Well, you up for it, beautiful?"

Kelsey glanced in Nikki's direction, the abrupt tension in her lithe frame awkward as hell. Wrench dealt out another hand, the snap of cards too loud—

"Absolutely," she said, turning with a breathtaking smile.

Grim stood and held out a hand. She took it, leading him to one of the booths and pulling the curtain shut.

Listen for Nikki

—game?—

Yeah, it's a game. We're gonna see how bad we can piss the bitch off.

[KEEN INTEREST]

Grim sat in the straight-backed chair, legs spread wide. Kelsey started to dance. Damn, he'd love to draw this out, but they didn't have time. He shook his head, patting his thigh. "Come here, baby."

Kelsey licked her lips, straddling it. "I didn't think you did this kind of thing."

"I don't." He weighed her breast in his hand, thumb flicking off the star. Beneath it, her pale pink nipple was beaded. "But I really wanna suck your tits. That okay with you?" Grim tugged on it, eyes on her lips.

She wet them, nodding, rising up to meet his lowered face. He licked across her nipple, drawing it into his mouth with a long, slow pull. It hardened against his tongue, and he groaned, pulling at the other and nipping lightly. "Fuck, you're beautiful."

Kelsey's fingers wove through his hair, her arousal spicing the small space. She moved to straddle his lap, his hands kneading her ass cheeks as he suckled her tits.

"You wet for me, baby?" His fingers skated over the gusset of her panties.

"Oh God, so wet. You have no idea how hard I fuck myself thinking about you," she rocked against him, her lips dropping to capture his. Grim's tongue invaded her sweet mouth, and she groaned, sucking on it. "This is like a dream or something…"

"Yeah? Tell me you want my cock," he murmured, pulling away to nip at her jaw. He slid his fingers into her ripe pussy, and she moaned, riding his hand. Woman was fucking soaked.

"I do, I want it."

"I wanna give it to you."

"Right here?" Kelsey threw her head back, pulling at her tits, nipples rock hard points.

"Mmm. Unless you know someplace better."

She tensed, then shook her head. "No. Here is good."

—lie—

Yeah, whatever's going on, the mollys know about it and don't want me to. "Here?" His thumb circled her clit, and she bit back a cry.

"Oh God, yes…"

You hear Nikki yet?

—getting closer—

"Take out my cock, baby."

My dick needs to be hard when she finds us.

—…—

I swear I'm not gonna fuck her cunt, Darke—

Grim moaned at the rush of blood to his dick as the molly freed it from his jeans, stroking. His eyes rolled back with a sharp inhale. Kelsey dropped to her knees, tongue traveling around his crown, lapping up his pre-cum, teeth tugging on his piercing. "Jesus fuck, that feels good…"

—*Mmm*—

Yeah…we should do this more often, asshole.

—…—

Kelsey gripped the base of his dick, hollowing her cheeks and bobbing. Grim moaned again, hand in her hair. His cock hit the back of her throat, and his balls tightened. Fuck, too long… it'd been too damned—

She popped off his cock, licking sloppy, base to lip. "When I touch myself, I think about you fucking my face."

—…—

Shut up. I'm fucking her face. He scooted forward, fisting her hair and driving his hips up. "Like this?"

Kelsey's fingers dug into his thighs, gagging around him as he thrust and humming her approval on the retreat. The scent of her arousal was so thick, he could taste it. "That's it. Open your throat like a good little whore and swallow my cock. I want your fingers in your pussy while you do."

Her hand slipped down between her legs, and she moaned.

"That's it, fuck yourself."

Twin streaks of mascara bled down her cheeks, eyes watering as he pumped his cock down her throat. Her breathing sped, mewling around his dick, tensing, then a splash of honey hitting the floor as she came. Fuck, that was so fucking hot… his dick pulsed, balls drawing up—

—*cum slut*—

"I gonna—fuck—swallow it—" His balls emptied out,

long ropes of molten, glistening white. She coughed, choking on it, and he pulled her off his dick, into his lap. Grim licked himself from her mouth, stroking the last of his release from his still hard cock between her ass cheeks. "You want more baby—

The curtain jerked back.

"The fuck, Grim!?" Nikki screeched half a second before her eyes locked on his erection. She gasped, stumbling back and giving the entire room front-row seat to his cum-coated dick. Kelsey's runny mascara and bee-stung lips, leaving no doubt as to how it'd gotten that way.

—*good game*—

A woman clapped and more joined her. Deuce whistled back at the table, him and Wrench laughing their asses off.

Kelsey hid her face against his throat. He stroked her hair, raising an eyebrow. "You mind?" He motioned to the curtain, running a hand down his sticky shaft.

"You're—" Nikki shook with rage. "It's—You—"

—*laughing*—

Grim patted Kelsey's thigh for her to get up. "Give me a sec," he murmured into her ear. "Do not go anywhere without me. We're not done." She gave a faint nod as he stood, leisurely tucking his cock away. Why rush? Most of the room had already gotten a good long look at it. Shit, more than a few assholes had their phones out, recording.

"What d'you want?"

Her nostrils flared. "You fucking came," she hissed. "With *her*."

"Yeah, and I plan on doing it again—" He turned like he was about to leave, then paused. "Oh, hey, while I gotcha, Clay wanted me to pass on a message. If you don't tone it the fuck down, and stop causing issues with the club, you're gone," Her face paled, and Grim leaned close. "But you do you. I'm looking forward to seeing how that works out."

—*good GOOD game*—

Glad you approve. Maybe you'll let me get head more often.

—…—

Fucker. He motioned to Kelsey, and she hurried to his side as strode to the main entrance.

"Wait, I can't leave, I'm still on the clock—"

"You can and you will," he said, holding the door open and pushing her outside basically naked. "Scholarship, right?"

She stumbled to keep up with his long stride, looking at him like he'd grown another head. "Um, yeah, but—"

"No buts, you drive here?"

Kelsey made a frustrated noise. "Yes, but my keys and clothes are all inside!"

"Sec." Grim pulled out his phone, dialing Triss and explaining shit. He shoved the phone at Kelsey. "Tell her what you need and how to get it. She'll bring it out."

Kelsey took the phone, wide-eyed and murmuring, glancing at him askance. She was shaking when she handed the phone back to Grim.

"Which one's your car?"

"That blue sedan," she said, pointing to the back corner of the lot.

He grunted, starting in that direction. Kelsey ran to catch up, and her heel catching on a rail line. Grim swore at her cry and swept her up in his arms.

"Are you always this chivalrous?"

"Hardly," he muttered. "Everyone will tell you I'm a miserable dick and dumb as fuck… but I'm glad you think I'm a good guy."

She gasped, her cheeks pinking beneath the parking lot lights. "Oh my God, you heard me talking to Becca, didn't you?"

"She the brunette?"

Kelsey nodded.

"Then, yeah, I did."

They made it to the end of the lot and Grim set her down on the trunk of her car. He cracked his wallet and handed her all the cash he had.

"What? No, I can't—"

"Yeah, you can." He'd planned on paying the club's tab, but fuck it. "Just shut up and take it. You need more, call the garage and leave Wrench—only Wrench—your number. Tell him you know Allie and make up a name, okay?"

Kelsey nodded dumbly, fingering the bills. "Why are you doing this?"

"Because I'm an asshole for using you like that, and your friend is right about Nikki ruining your life. Sooner you disappear, the better. I'm sorry, but I figured since you were leaving anyway… look, you earned it, okay?"

Her face went crimson. "I'm not—"

"Not what?"

Kelsey laughed. "I was gonna say, I'm not a whore, but…" She shrugged, biting her lip.

"You're not. You're just in a shit situation. Where'd you get accepted?"

"Uni at St. Lawrence." A smile ghosted over her lips. "I got into the Paranormal Studies program."

"Congrats."

There was a squeal behind them, and Triss ran over, shoving a bag at Kelsey and throwing herself at Grim. Wrench and Deuce trailed behind her.

"That. Was. Amazing!" She panted.

Grim shrugged, feeling like a dick about the whole thing, even if seeing the look on Nikki's face was fucking epic. He'd definitely put her into reactive mode, but taking her down a peg didn't change the fact that he needed to talk to Clay about Deacon.

"I should get going." Kelsey had pulled on a sweatshirt and was holding her keys. She kissed Grim's cheek. "Thank you."

He snorted. "For what?"

"For being a good guy." She smiled and got into her car.

Grim stepped back, watching her drive away.

"You know you just kicked up a shit storm, right?" Deuce asked. Wrench grunted his agreement.

"Nah," Grim scratched at his jaw. "I mean, no good's gonna come of it, but the storm was already here. I need to get back to the club. You guys staying?"

Wrench snorted. "Way Nikki's losing her shit in there? No fucking thank you." He wasn't the only one of that opinion. People were exiting the club like a concert had just ended.

"I was gonna take Triss home, then head back myself." Deuce glowered like he was daring one of them to say something about that. Triss beamed, hooking her arm through his.

Nope, no comment.

"Right. I'll see you guys there, then." Grim kissed Triss's forehead and went to find his bike. Maybe something good would come out of tonight after all.

Forty-five minutes later, Grim pulled into the clubhouse's lot. Inside was quiet, music a low hum, bar devoid of mollys. A few old timers sat around drinking. Hanna was drying glasses behind it. She raised an eyebrow as he plonked down onto a stool.

"You're back early," she said, filling a glass for him.

"Not really my scene." He took the drink she slid over to him, grateful for the burn.

Hanna shook her head, her shoulder length grey hair bobbing. "I can't figure you out, kid. Drives my cat crazy." He raised an eyebrow, and she leaned against the bar, tossing the towel over her shoulder. "Long as you've been here, you don't so much as look at a molly, then you go and pull that shit tonight. The hell were you thinking?"

He winced, taking another sip. "Already heard about that, huh?"

"Heard? I saw the damned videos." She shook her head. "Nikki's in a fucking lather."

"Good. She should be."

Hanna's face went hard. "Oh. It's like that, huh? Just figured you could use Kelsey in whatever fucked up game the two of you are playing?"

Grim didn't answer, finishing his drink.

"Let me tell you something, Grimdarke James, them mollys might've signed up for getting bent over by the lot of you assholes, but they sure as hell didn't sign up for having their lives ruined in the process, and as long as you're tangled up with that vindictive bitch the rest of them are off fucking limits. You got me?"

—bad game—

[SHAME]

Had to be done. He pursed his lips, twisting his glass in its condensation ring on the bar.

Hanna spat out a disgusted growl at his silence and stormed into the back room.

Grim left his glass on the bar and made his way to Clay's office, rapping a knuckle against the door before pushing it open. His father was at his desk with a bottle, old photos spread out before him.

"Grim." He glanced up at him, shuffling the photos into a pile and turning them face down. "Have a seat, son. I could use the company. Drink?"

"Yeah, sure," he said, settling into the chair across from his father.

Clay snagged another glass from the desk's bottom drawer and poured him a generous amount. "Hear you got a future in film."

"Saw that, did you?"

Clay snorted, sipping on his whiskey. "Pretty sure the whole damned internet saw that," he said, glancing at Grim's lap. "You wanna tell me what the point of getting caught with your pants down was?"

"Wasn't a planned thing," he muttered, taking the glass.

"Bullshit."

That it was. Moving on, "You know about the setup Deacon's got in the back of the Cat House?"

His father's face went blank. Goddamn it, the fucker did. "Better question is, what do you know about it."

Grim shrugged, trying to play it off like he didn't care. "Not much more than I saw."

"He let you back there?" The note of surprise in Clay's voice set Grim's jaw.

"No. Heard some prospects talking at the door, keeping an eye out for me. Wanted to find out why… I went in through the roof and landed in the middle of it."

His father grunted. "Shit ain't sanctioned, MC receives zero profits, and neither of us know about it, got me?" He frowned at Grim's expression, fingers brushing against his pile of photos.

"But the prospects and the mollys do."

"In for a penny, in for a pound," Clay muttered, scrubbing at his face. "Since you ain't gonna drop this, I didn't know about the prospects, but yeah, the mollys working there know. So does Hanna. She was keeping tabs through them, Kelsey in-fucking-particular, which is why your stunt tonight is a serious pain in my ass. Nikki's created such a divide between the ol' ladies and the mollys, Hanna doesn't know who she can trust to replace her."

"Try Becca."

His father raised an eyebrow.

"I overheard some shit between her and Kelsey. She's not a fan of Nikki, who's fucking Deacon, by the way."

Clay threw back the last of what was in his glass and poured another. "Not surprised."

"What's the endgame here, Clay?

"I'm just doling out the rope, son. I gave Deacon fair warning at table. He wants to hang himself with it, far be it from me to stop him."

"You don't think that'll blow back on the club if the Feds raid the place?"

Clay pursed his lips. "I've taken steps to ensure it don't, but it still could. Which is why all this divisive shit needs to stop. You give Nikki my message?"

"Yeah, right after she found me with Kelsey."

"Didn't take you for a showman." His father chuckled. "But I suspect that got the point across. Nikki needs to understand we got rules, and she needs to follow them. She wants to act like a molly, I can't fault you for treating her like one."

"Hanna can," he muttered. "She all but threatened to cut my dick off if I did anything like that again."

"Hanna's in a shit situation. MC doesn't have a queen. She's doing the best she can, but doesn't have the political clout to make it happen with Nikki's pushback. Rest of the mollys jumping on board is insult to fucking injury."

Grim scraped a hand along his stubbled jaw. "So why not take one?"

"A queen?" His father's fingers ghosted to the pictures again. "I tried, and I'm not going there again." He swept the pile into a drawer, his expression turning to business.

"Russians are amenable to our terms if we can make the arms drop tomorrow. Deal wasn't for as much as I wanted, but it gets us free and clear, and they've got a witch who'll look at MK's leg. Braintrust over at Union General can't do shit for him. You're running point. Take the usual crew."

Grim frowned. "We're down two men. Wrench is gimping around and Deuce can't hold a gun." Not to mention his fucked up shoulder, but he'd deal.

"Shanghai Stitch and Brick."

"Stitch?" Brick would be an asset, but the sergeant at arms wasn't exactly field material anymore. Grim wasn't sure what a doped up mug-shot Santa was gonna contribute if things went sideways.

"Yeah, Stitch." Clay chuckled. "Man can charm the pants of Satan himself, and whether you know it or not, he's got your back. That girl of his thinks you hung the moon, especially after you let her work on your bike."

"She's got little fingers," he muttered.

"What she's got is more sway around here than you think. If Deuce would just get his head out of his ass, she'd make a fine ol' lady, and my life a hell of a lot easier."

Grim snorted, not fucking likely, but… "He took her home tonight."

"Good." Clay rolled the edge of his glass on the desk. "When you get back, we need to make a run into the city."

Grim bit back a groan. "Council shit?"

Clay chuckled again, polishing off his whiskey. "Nope, you're off the hook there."

"You gonna elaborate, or is it a surprise?"

"Oh, it's a fucking surprise all right. That shit you were spewing about responding rather than reacting's got me thinking… might be time to add some of my own fuckery into the mix. Get some sleep, son. Four hours to Westchester County is gonna come early after tonight."

Grim stood, throwing back his glass of untouched whiskey. That it fucking was.

CHAPTER FOUR

GRIM GRIPPED the wheel of the SUV, squirming against the leather seat. Damn, he hated driving a cage, but no way was his shoulder up for a four-hour ride, and the weather had turned nasty about an hour out. Brothers on bikes were having a shit time of it. MK probably was too. They'd loaded him into the back of one of the vans, doped up out of his mind, but the man had still whimpered like a baby when they were getting him settled.

The merchandise had been split between what Grim was driving and three other vehicles, arms hidden away in compartments built into the undercarriages and back seats. Fit was tight, but hauling crates seemed like another level of stupid.

But then, none of this felt right.

Beside him, Stitch cracked the window and pulled out his vape. Grim glanced at the clock on the dash. Was the fourth time in the past fifteen minutes. Man had to be high as a kite.

"How's the shoulder?"

"Still attached." Grim frowned, hitting his blinker and moving into the left lane. Semi he was behind had a busted mud flap and the asshole driving kept riding the brakes.

Stitch chuckled, taking a hit. Was that an old man thing? Between him and Clay, it could've been a canned response.

"Triss was saying you tore a bunch of stitches out. Doc was pissed as shit."

"Doc's always pissed."

"True that." Stitch said, far too cheerfully. Must be where Triss got it from. "I wanted t'thank you for the other day. Triss's been in her head lately, pinin' over that dumbass friend of yours. Workin' on your bike did her good…" Man's oyster grey eyes went flinty. "Can't say I was pleased when he brought her home last night."

Grim glanced at him askance. Well, this was awkward as fuck. "Deuce isn't—"

"Like hell he ain't. Pheromones don't fucking lie, so I'd suggest you cut the shit."

Grim's hands tightened on the wheel. "I was gonna say, he's not planning on acting on them. Thinks Triss is too young."

"She is." Stitch growled.

All righty then.

"Now that we're clear on that, tell me about this cluster-fuck with Nikki."

"What about it?" Grim gritted out.

"Weren't you listenin' t'what I just said about pheromones? Might have the rest of the brothers fooled, but you hate the bitch, so what's this bull about you makin' her your queen?"

Sweat bloomed on Grim's brow.

"You can fess up now or when I piss in your Cheerios and sway the table enough t'nix whatever deal you've got goin'." The old man shrugged. "Your choice."

"This why Clay wanted me to haul around your fat ass today?"

Cue the chuckle. Grim's teeth clenched so hard his teeth popped.

"Nah. Your daddy's always been a big picture man, but the details," Stitch tapped the side his nose. Too bad there wasn't a chimney for him to disappear into, "that's where I come in. Rest of 'em couldn't sniff out a fart if someone lit it on fire. So spill, what's she got on you?"

Grim scowled, smacking the radio on and changing lanes, Tom Petty blaring out.

"I'm guessing it's got somewhat t'do with your rumored erectile disfunction," Stitch mused over the music. " 'Course, you put that t'bed—pun intended—last night. Smart, doin' it so publicly."

Grim's head snapped over to stare at the man.

Stitch toked on his vape like he hadn't just dropped a bomb. He cleared the carb and shrugged. "Doc and I talk. Add in those nightmares you had after comin' back t'two legs, way you act around the mollys, then flashing your junk around…" He exhaled. "Pieces fit. Nice crown piercing, by the way. That takes some balls."

Jesus H. Christ. Grim pinched across his temples. Being stuck in a cage having a heart to heart about his dick was not where he wanted to be.

Fuck. "Does Clay know about this theory of yours?"

Stitch frowned. "No, and if the details are anything like I'm imaging, shit would kill him."

"I guarantee they're worse, and that's what Nikki's got on me," Grim muttered.

"You spilled t'her?"

He shook his head, and Stitch hummed under his breath, vape tapping against his knee, counter to the beat blaring from the speakers. Free falling in-fucking-deed.After a few minutes, Stitch smacked the radio off.

"So the bitch is blackmailing you t'make her queen, while doing everything she possibly can t'assure that don't happen."

"Basically." Grim sighed, running a hand through his hair.

"Don't make no goddamned sense."

"Nope."

"Unless she ain't actually after being queen."

Grim snorted. "Nikki wants power. The fuck else would get her it?"

"That's the question, ain't it?" Stitch mused. "Think she could be one of them spies?"

The thought had crossed Grim's mind, but Nikki wasn't stupid. She wouldn't be working with Reaper, she'd be working for him, and the bitch wasn't one to take direction. She'd have her own agenda... but if the two aligned...

"I dunno. He's been locked up for a hell of a lot longer than she's been around—"

"Your brothers ain't."

Grim's jaw tightened. The subject of his brothers wasn't one he liked to dwell on. Despite the three of them being born at the same time, they only shared a mother. Like true cats, female shifters could be concurrently impregnated by multiple males. Shiv and Grapple were twins, whereas Grim... well, he was the shit left over.

And they'd made sure he knew it.

He scratched his jaw. His oldest brother, Shiv—shit, he and Nikki were two peas in a goddamned pod, and Grim couldn't see Grapple being a deal breaker. His brothers had always shared their conquests, whether the woman was on board with it or not.

Grim was pretty sure that wouldn't be a deterrent for Nikki.

Assholes had been keeping a low profile after Reaper got pinched for attempted murder, and Grim hadn't gone looking for them. Last he knew, Shiv had taken over as Satan's Vengeance's prez in Reaper's absence, and Grapple was his enforcer. The MC was heavily involved in drug running about an hour away in La Farge.

Was it possible they'd hooked up with Nikki? Yeah. Likely? Grim wasn't sure.

"I'll take your silence as it being a possibility," Stitch said, derailing his train of thought.

Grim sighed, changing his grip on the steering wheel. "Yeah, I guess. Shiv is pretty fucking smooth when he wants to be. Grapple usually blows that to shit, but..." He chewed his lip, mulling it over.

"No." Grim shook his head. "Something about it's off. Sure, SV wants to wipe us off the map and take over the gun trade. But they've got half our numbers, and the council fucking hates Reaper along with most of his crew. Damn MC's made up of every exile and reject in the Eastern United States. Even if Maw of Mayhem ceased to exist, they wouldn't hold a fraction of the clout we do now. No way Nikki would sign up for that."

"Well, then we're back to her being a psychotic cunt," Stitch said around his vape as Grim hit his blinker for the exit. "Good thing you've got experience handling her, we're about t'meet more."

Wasn't what Grim wanted to hear.

The witch's compound was a huge gated affair, because of course it fucking was. He'd say they got groceries in Prada, but they had people to do that shit for them. He pulled up to the entrance for deliveries and stopped at the guard shack, which was way closer to a summer cottage in the Hamptons than a lean-to in the Appalachians. Dogs somewhere on the grounds started going apeshit about three seconds after he rolled down his window.

Most likely because they'd been trained to run down shifters. God, he hated witches.

A dude who was so ex-military elite he smelled like gun oil and MREs checked Grim's ID, then got on comms to "verify their clearance level."

Grim rolled his eyes. Like anyone was gonna gatecrash a fucking coven. Well, not without good reason. The four brothers on bikes had peeled off after the exit just in case shit went down and they needed backup.

Despite the rain, another jarhead wheeled around a mirror on a stick, inspecting their undercarriages. Wasn't a terrible idea, considering. He gave a nod, and the dude checking comms directed them to the carriage house, whatever the fuck that was. They drove up a long gravel drive lined by massive oaks.

The main house was at the top of the rise. The back had three stories, a massive porch with white columns, and perfectly manicured landscaping wrapping around what Grim was pretty sure was a pool. Tennis courts were set off to the left.

Must be fucking nice.

Ahead was what he assumed was the carriage house. Looked like a super fancy eight car garage to him, but what the fuck did he know? Four of the bays were open, and a guy in a three-piece suit waving a blinking traffic baton was motioning for them to pull in.

Dipshit.

Grim pulled a U-ey and backed the SUV into one of the spaces, the rest of the vehicles following suit.

The garage doors closed and fur sprouted on the back of his neck.

"Easy, kid," Stitch murmured, unbuckling his seat belt. "Assholes get off on this shit."

Grim grunted, climbing out of the cage. A witch wearing a pale pink pants suit greeted them. Pearls in her ears were as big as grapes. She sashayed over, a smug smile her face.

He already didn't like her.

"You must be Grimdarke," she said, with a low Eastern European lilt, his name coming out as "Greemderk."

"Who wants to know?"

"Aelita Rostrova," her smile didn't falter as she rolled her Rs, "your coven liaison with the Bratva for this exchange. If you'd be so kind as to unload the goods into the receptacles on the far wall—"

"Sure, soon as I see numbers in my account."

The witch's green eyes glittered, and traffic baton guy shuffled into view behind her. "Ah. My mistress mentioned you might make this onerous. I'm afraid we'll need to inspect what you've brought before an exchange can be made—unless you'd care to leave now."

Grim's knuckles popped and Stitch ambled forward.

"Aelita, was it? If memory serves, name means starlight seen for the last time."

She blinked at him like an owl. "You know Tolstoy?"

"Honey, I know a little bit of everything. Call me Stitch, everybody do, and I'd be happy t'pull out a little somethin' for you t'see." He took her elbow and directed her to the back of the SUV, yapping some shit about Russian literature.

Traffic baton guy stayed where he was, glowering.

Grim ignored him and, after a moment, followed the other two, a hand raking through his hair. Damn it, he wasn't cut out for this shit. By the time he caught up with them, Stitch had opened the haul, and Aelita was peering down the sights of an AR-15. She was pressed back against his bulk, and his hand was on her hip.

"Yeah, that's right, set the stock in that hollow of your shoulder. Good girl... ya' feel it?"

The witch giggled.

What the fuck?

Stitch glanced up at Grim and winked. He stepped back from her with a light slap to her rear. "How 'bout we go outside and pop off some rounds?"

"Oh! N-no," she stammered, handing him back the gun and tucking a lock of cinnamon hair behind her ear. "I couldn't possibly. It would be terribly disruptive for my mistress's guests... but I do appreciate the offer." She turned to Grim, her cheeks flushed, and took out her phone, thumb tapping over the screen.

"The agreed-upon amount has been transferred. If you'd please verify?"

Grim pulled up his app and grunted. "We're good. And MK?"

"Ah, yes, your injured brethren. One moment."

Aelita quickly texted something, the brothers unloading the arms into the "receptacles," which equated to crates with fancy foam cutouts. Something flashed across her screen, and her face paled.

"What's wrong, honey?" Stitch asked.

"M-master Shamir will be with you shortly. He doesn't—" Aelita licked her lips and visibly collected herself. "His attention honors you."

Grim's eyebrow quirked. Unless there was more than one of them, Shamir was also the Queen Witch's baby-daddy, and from what Grim had heard, an anomaly. Man was supposed to be the most powerful magic user on the continent, a title usually held by a woman. But far stranger was the rumor he didn't give two shits about it, letting his wife rule over their paranormal sect while he meditated or some shit.

The hair on Grim's nape prickled.

The look on Stitch's face said his was doing the same.

Grim forced a smile. "We'll be sure to thank him."

Aelita glanced in his direction, her nose wrinkling like she suddenly smelled dog shit. "Be sure you do." She turned her back on him and wandered over to micromanage the brothers transferring the goods.

"You catch that?" Stitch asked, watching her rear sway as she left. No wonder him and Doc were always on the outs. Forget about a tom, man was a dog.

"Which part? Your bizarre knowledge of Russian literature, or the impending visit from the Witch King?"

"Chicks dig men that can quote 'em shit." He chuckled,

pulling out his vape. "But I was referring to the incoming royalty. He's supposed t'be eccentric." Stitch raised his brow, not fucking around. "Play along with him."

Grim nodded, a hand running down his face as his cat perked up.

—game?—

No. Not a game. I've gotta humor the son of a bitch so he doesn't fry us. Grim jammed his hands in his pockets, not fucking happy about the turn of events. Stitch exhaled his hit and offered him the vape. Shit was tempting...

Aelita's head whipped around, her eyes bulbous. "Oh! Sir —eh, Stitch, please, you can't—"

"Peace, child." A golden skinned man appeared in the space between them where he sure as hell hadn't been a second ago.

—magic—

Shit. Yeah. That had to be Shamir.

—is a game—

A fuzzy visual of a man-sized whack-a-mole came from his cat, and Grim bit back a snort. *No. Go back to sleep.*

Aelita curtsied low. "Yes, my master, but, the mistress—"

"Is not here." He dismissed Aelita with a wave of his long-fingered hand, his attention riveting on Grim.

Grim was riveted by the man's fancy silk pajamas.

—spell—

His cat hissed when he didn't respond.

—MINE!—

An etherial claw swiped at something, and Grim winced. He shook his head, abruptly free of whatever that was, and took a step back. His stomach dropped. Stitch and the rest of the crew stood frozen.

Shamir was smiling like he was ridiculously pleased. Shit. Maybe this was a game.

His cat's tail twitched.

"How incredibly delightful... I have to say, I didn't expect that, and I'm so very rarely surprised." Shamir ran a hand down his embroidered silk tunic to tap his fingers against his abs. The shimmery blue fabric stopped just below his knee. Wide-legged emerald pants flowed from below it, and his feet were bare. Getup was chichi as hell.

"It's called a kurta."

Grim raised a brow. "A what?"

"A kurta. Traditional garb from South Asia. Granted, this is much finer than the ones I wore in my youth, but my wife insists I dress the part. I find its familiarity comforting. But don't tell her that, lest she decide a lungi would be more appropriate."

"I—Uh, yeah." Not a clue what he was talking about and wasn't interested in the CliffsNotes.

Shamir's smile widened. "Let's begin again. I am Shamir Dhar, master of this coven, King Witch to the uninitiated, and overall inconvenience to my sect. And you are?"

"Grimdarke James, ah, just Grim," he said, shoving his fists deeper into his pockets.

"I don't believe you're *just* anything, especially not with that remarkable beast behind your eyes." Shamir waggled his fingers in an affected wave. "Hello in there."

[ANNOYANCE]

Grim's brow furrowed, and Shamir laughed.

"Aside from that, you're vice president of the Maw of Mayhem MC, yes?"

"Yeah." Grim snapped, vibing with his cat. "Look, I appreciate you coming personally to heal MK, but whatever spell you've got my crew under—"

Shamir's eyes caught Grim's and time slowed. "That was two, but it's the third title that defines you, you know. Your role to play. Mine is to be a speed bump to ambition, but you…" His deep chocolate gaze sharpened and a grin sliced across his face. "Oh my. With the right push, what a marvelous opponent you'll become."

Shamir leaned close, his voice dropping to a whisper. "She's coming."

A golden fingertip pressed between Grim's brows, and everything went black.

—bad game—

Grim started, the seatbelt of the SUV's passenger seat locking at his sudden movement.

Stitch glanced over at him. "You all right there, Sleeping Beauty?"

"The fuck happened?" he asked, fumbling for the flask in his jacket. His mouth was dry as hell, and goddamn, that'd been some freaky shit.

"You tell me. One minute Shamir pops into the garage, the next you're on the floor. Man stepped over you, healed MK, and we got the fuck outta Dodge. Good thing Brick was with us, your ass is a hell of a lot heavier than it looks."

Grim scrubbed over his face, head pounding, the details fleeting, like a dream. "I spoke with him. Some shit about three titles and speed bumps…"

—opponent—

"Told ya Shamir was eccentric."

"That code for insane asshole?"

Stitch snickered. "Witches is a whole different breed, kid. S'how they come straight outta the box. He must've liked you."

"The fuck makes you say that?"

"You're still breathing. I ain't never felt power like I did when he healed MK. Bled all over the garage. My arthritis ain't been this clear in years."

Grim paused, flask halfway to his lips. Shit, his shoulder didn't ache either. He pushed over the neck of his T and flicked off the bandage. Not a damned mark. You'd think Shamir could've done something for his head… unless he'd done something *to* his head—

—no, stayed out—

Cat said it too quick, like he was hiding something. *He say something to you?*

—...—

Asshole.

The ride back was miserable, a full-blown migraine blooming in the wake of their visit. By the time they hit the compound, Grim was seeing halos around everything and felt like he was gonna puke. He stumbled through the clubhouse up to his room. His sheets were rucked up in a pile in front of the door and smelled like they'd been pissed on.

Probably because they had.

He kicked them aside and rushed into the bathroom, heaving his guts. Fuck this fucking shit. He moaned, his steps weaving across the bedroom to fall onto his bare mattress, arm over his eyes, wishing he could just pass the fuck out.

Someone swore softly, and the door scraped against the floor, too damned loud.

"Grim. Open up and take these."

Triss. Two pills slipped between his parted lips, and he crunched on them. Jagged lines of agony shot through his skull. The sound of the shades being pulled, and the room darkened. Boots pulled from his feet, pockets emptied. Afghan tucking around him.

"What's the door code?"

"1-2-1-6," he murmured, wincing.

A feather-light kiss landed on his brow. "I'll be back to check on you."

The door clicked behind her.

Grim lay there in misery, pills slowly taking the edge off. He curled up, nose buried in his afghan, starting to drift...

...she's coming...

Shamir's words slid through his mind, a sinuous whisper echoing meaninglessly. His cat batted at them, chasing them away only for them to pop up somewhere else.

—bad game—

Yeah, buddy. It sure as fuck was.

———

Triss checked in as promised, feeding him more pills and making him drink water. She somehow managed to get clean sheets on the bed, but then, she knew her business. Girl had been working at the vet's her whole life.

When Grim woke up feeling marginally human, Clay was in the room, sprawled out in the recliner, looking like he hadn't slept. Grim glanced at his phone. 3pm. He'd slept all damned day and most of the next.

"How you feelin', son?" Clay nodded to a cup of luke-warm coffee on the bedside table. "Triss said caffeine might help."

Grim grunted his thanks and sat up to grab it, his clothes from the day before damp with sweat.

"So… I hear you met Shamir."

He eyed Clay over the rim of his mug. His father's lips pursed like he wasn't necessarily pleased about that. Whelp, that made two of them. "Yeah."

"Bastard did in my head once, too."

"He say a bunch of fucked up shit while he was at it?"

Clay tensed. "Yes, and he laughed like a maniac after I punched him for it."

Grim snorted. Wished he'd gotten the opportunity.

"Why? What'd he say to you?" his father asked.

"Can't really remember much," Grim said, sipping his coffee.

—lie—

Fuck off. You won't come clean, why should I?

—…—

"What do you remember?" Clay pressed.

"Something about him being a general inconvenience to his sect and a speed bump for ambition."

"Well, that's fucking accurate," his father muttered, sitting back and running a hand over his beard. "Interesting that he's aware of it. Witches touched by prophecy are usually pretty removed from—"

"He's a prophet?"

Clay snorted. "Asshole once bet me fifty bucks the next person to sit at the bar we were at would get shit on by a bird. Mind you, this was indoors after one of those big council meets. I figured he was plastered like the rest of us and took him up on it. Five minutes later, a vamp walks in with a parrot on his shoulder, pulls up a seat, and the damn bird craps down the front of his shirt." His father's knuckles knocked on the arm of the recliner.

"Either Shamir gets glimpses of the future, or he's powerful enough to make it happen. Witches ain't confirmin' or denyin' either way, but since then, my money's been on both." Clay took a breath, sucking in his cheeks before he spoke again.

"You don't wanna tell me everything that went down, fine, but surer than shit, he singled you out for a reason. I suggest you think on what he said, 'cause now the rest of his miserable sect is gonna be hot to find out why."

Well, wasn't that just tits.

Clay's expression closed up. He tugged on his beard and stood. "I got some work to do. Get cleaned up. I'd like to head into the city around five."

Motherf—"We're still going?"

"Yeah. I've put it off too long."

Grim raked a hand through his hair and nodded. Once Clay set his mind to something, there wasn't any changing it. His father left, and Grim took a shower, his head still not right. Ride was gonna suck.

Triss was curled up in the recliner, scrolling through her phone when he came out, a towel wrapped around his waist.

"Do I need to change the door's code again?"

"Only if you wanna get your own food," she said, nodding to a plate loaded down with a burger and fries on his nightstand.

Damn, that looked good. Grim grunted, grabbing a pair of sweats and changing in the bathroom before coming out and attacking it. Triss's brow furrowed at the little screen, bottom lip pinched between her teeth.

"What I miss?" he asked, not really wanting to know.

"Feds raided the Cat House last night after the video of you went viral. Deacon's in lockup with a dozen plus mollys, and Clay's letting them stew. A bunch of suits were here earlier, confiscated Miser's books and a bunch of records. It's divine frickin' providence you made that run, they were crawling all over the place—"

"Nikki get pinched?"

"Nope," Triss said, popping the P. "Nobody's seen her since she freaked out the other night."

Grim frowned, chewing on a fry. Where had Nikki slithered off to now? Wasn't like she had any friends that would put her up... though several of the brothers had houses off site—She could be shacked up with one of them.

Damn, shit was hitting the fan, but fuck Nikki. Better question was why Clay still wanted to go into the city. What the hell could be so goddamned important he was gonna leave the club while the Feds were sniffing around?

"That's frickin' amazing." Triss's eyes were on Grim's shoulder. "Stitch said that witch healed it, but—there's not even a scar. Unbelievable. You know, Doc told me once that when we had a True Queen over all the shifters, we used to heal crazy fast. I didn't believe her, but seeing that... you think it's possible?"

Grim looked down, rolling his arm in the socket. "Yeah, maybe." A hundred fucking years ago when fairies supposedly existed.

Triss frowned at him. "Just because we don't have one

now, doesn't mean we never will again." She cleared her throat and sat up straight, reciting. "To every century—"

He snorted, and she stuck out her tongue at him. "Yeah, yeah, and if you do the math, the new century started like, twenty something years ago. It's bullshit, Triss. Or maybe the coven and the vamps snuffed this one like they did the last."

"Mmm. I don't think the vamps would," she said, chewing her lip. "They weren't real pleased about the way things turned out after they stabbed us in the back. The coven really fucked them over... not that retaliating by instigating the whole Salem thing was small potatoes, but still."

Grim took a bite of his burger. "True that," he said around his mouthful. "Man, you shoulda seen their layout. Coven's rolling in dough. Fucked up to think shifters were just as loaded back in the day." Whether or not the healing thing was legit, their slow slide from prosperity sure as hell was. Without a True Queen, their sect had splintered, and it was every species of shifter for themselves. The infighting had halved their numbers and bankrupted them.

They still hadn't recovered.

Triss came over and sat beside him, stealing one of his fries. "You talk in your sleep."

His stomach clenched. "Yeah? I say anything good?"

"I dunno... depends on who *she* is, I guess."

Shit. "She?"

"Yeah, as in, she's coming." Triss's eyes got a wicked glimmer, and she started moaning in a high falsetto, "Oh, Grim! Grim, Mmm, I'm coming! Oh! I'm coming!"

"Get the fuck out." He laughed, chucking a fry at her.

Triss blew him a kiss and ducked through the door.

He shoved the last of his burger into his mouth and checked the time on his phone. Was already quarter after four. He still couldn't believe he'd slept through the whole damned day. Not that he minded missing all the excitement with the Feds.

What a clusterfuck. Grim pulled on a pair of jeans and a henley. No doubt Clay had already lawyered up, and not posting bail would broadcast his displeasure with Deacon. Especially after the county courthouse had burnt down. For anything more serious than a speeding ticket or drunk and disorderly, arrests got detained in a holding cell at the prison and a taste of gen pop. Wasn't exactly homey.

And the Feds weren't completely stupid. They'd take that as a clear sign Deacon no longer had the club's backing, which would translate into them pressuring him to nark. Grim finished getting dressed, weighing the likelihood of that happening. Wasn't like this would be a quick six to eight, in and out. Even with a reduced sentence, man was probably looking at—

Shit.

He grabbed the rest of his gear and hauled ass to the basement of the club. Mouse was gaming in front of a huge flatscreen taking up the far wall, yelling commands into his headset and virtually blowing away zombies.

The tech nerd glanced at him, then back to his game, fingers flying over the controller. "Hey man, s'up?"

"I need a list of all the police detainees sent to County Corrections along with the inmate intakes and discharges over the past decade."

"Psh—lemme hop right on it. You want that order super-sized while I'm—"

Mouse's fingers froze, and his screen flashed, simulated guts spattering everywhere.

"Holy fuck. You think that's how Reaper's getting messages out?" He ripped off the headset and jumped into his computer chair, skidding to a stop in front of his laptop. "That's fucking brilliant. Off the fucking wall, but brilliant. Any names in particular?"

"All known members and associates of Satan's Vengeance, and throw in the shitheads we know that are dealing for them, too," Grim said, adrenaline making his cat pace. "You get Lasik or something?"

"Hmm? Oh, no. I can see perfectly fine." Mouse murmured, focused on his screen. "Those glasses are blue light lenses. Totally a gimmick, but the mollys think they're hot as hell. You'd be surprised how many women have a nerd kink."

"Nikki one of them?"

Mouse snickered. "That molly's kink is kink—" His eyes flicked to Grim's and the tech nerd cringed. "I mean, so I hear."

"Bullshit, and I know you gave her the code to my door."

"Yeah, sorry about that, man. You were on a run, and she said she'd left her phone—"

"She didn't. Don't believe her shit about anything."

Mouse's eyes flicked to Grim's crotch. "Yeah, no worries there. She was definitely not on the up and up about your up and up. Brothers are pissed she spread that shit about you. You know, the whole virility thing was why half of them didn't want you patched in as VP... hey, you get that dydoe piercing in town?"

"No."

"Then where—"

"Montreal. She seriously ran her mouth about my cock?"

"Yeah, man. You know how girls talk. Word gets around. We figured it was true since you never party with us."

"It's not." Not totally, at least.

"So we saw."

Grim raked a hand through his hair. "How long will it take you to get me those lists?"

"I've already got the raw data, but I can't pull a clean CSV file out of it. Fucking ass backward government system—I'm gonna have to code something up to extract what you're looking for. Should have something by tomorrow morning, latest."

"Sooner the better."

Mouse gave a half-assed salute, already typing away.

Grim took the stairs up two at a time, then wandered into the bar to meet Clay. If that really was the way Reaper was communicating with his crew... shit, with all the petty drug charges and misdemeanors SV and their various dealers got picked up for on the reg, Reaper could've been talking to his crew on a daily basis...

Until he got tossed into solitary.

Grim pulled out a stool and sat, scratching his jaw. Three weeks ago. That woulda been about the same time the hits on their shipments had started. He sighed, still missing something.

Hanna came over with a glass of whiskey, her lips pursed. She fiddled with her towel as he took a sip. Liquor was top shelf instead of the usual shit she served him.

"We celebrating something?"

Hanna shrugged. "Might be I owe you an apology, if what you did ran that molly off for good and shut down that abomination of Deacon's."

"And if it didn't?"

"Then I'm still pissed at you."

He rolled a mouthful around. "Guess I'll take what I can get."

"I guess you better." She smirked, headed into the back.

Clay came out of his office a moment later, the lines on his face drawn. He pulled out the stool beside Grim, rolling his phone on the bar. "Mouse sent me a text. Think you might have the right of it. Can't believe Reaper was doing that right under our noses, I didn't even think twice about it when his crew got pinched for burning the courthouse down. Figured it was some dumb stunt—" He shook his head. "Man must be laughing his ass off."

"Probably," Grim said, savoring another sip. "Still doesn't

explain our shipments getting jacked right when Reaper went into solitary. Triss said the Feds were here?"

"Yeah. Heat's off us for now, but they'll be back."

"Always are. You gonna tell me what tonight's about?"

Clay's lips pursed. "I don't—you know Nikki ain't your queen."

"Remains to be seen. I know she's not my mate, but I don't believe in that shit."

"You should. Good Lord put someone out there for each of us. Sometimes it just takes us a bit to find 'em. When you do, I'd suggest you say fuck off to everything else you've got going on and hold on to her like she's your next breath. Air won't be worth dick and neither will anything else if you lose her."

Grim swirled the amber liquid in his glass, not wanting to think about what that meant as far as he was concerned. He threw the last of what was in his glass back, dregs tasting like shit.

"You ready to ride?"

Clay's jaw tightened. "Yeah. Let's do this."

CHAPTER FIVE

Meanwhile, in the city…

KIT GRIPPED her messenger bag closer, hurrying down the busy streets and cursing. She was gonna be late, again, but the overtime from closing out the last quarter at Hewllet, Detrond, and Lowey was currently paying the lion's share of her rent.

Her knock-off Vuittons pinched like a mother with each step, but the nude peep-toes looked fierce with her grey pencil skirt. Accounting wasn't glamorous, but she'd be damned before she dressed like Susan and Mallory. Bitches looked like extras from *Nine to Five*.

And with the tips Kit planned on making tonight at Skin, she could cover the rest of what that Hermes bag in hock was gonna cost her—Mmm! She could already feel the weight of the mocha calfskin Garden Purse on her shoulder—

A shadow moved at the mouth of the alley to her right, and goosebumps prickled over her skin. Assholes were back.

Just ignore it, Kit. They're not gonna do shit.

Fucking shifters had been darkening her door for weeks now. They hadn't made a move, but sure as hell liked to watch. Perverts. She'd read about shit like this, some caveman bull about them picking up on the pheromones of unaffiliated female shifters and becoming fixated or some shit. Couldn't act like normal people and ask her on a date, nooo... fucking animals had to stalk her. City must have a shortage if they were desperate enough to be coming out in force for a half-breed like her.

Like for real. One of them had been outside the bathrooms at Skin last weekend, smirking at her from the shadows like he knew something.

Which maybe he fucking did, but goddamn it, she didn't have time for their shit. No way was she gonna be the mouse to their cats.

She crossed the street to her building, keys in hand. The rent controlled co-op wasn't in the best part of the city, but it didn't have gang bangers hanging out in the front like her Aunt Jojo's place.

And there was a hell of a lot less judgement going on inside. No talk about Kit being spawned from the devil or her going to hell. Like she was evil just because her sperm donor was a piece of shifter shit. She'd rather sleep in a cardboard box than go back to that. Another lean shadow made itself known at the end of the hall, and she flipped it off before pushing into the apartment.

Mia had left the place a shithole. Her roommate's coke addiction was getting out of control. Wasn't so bad at first when she's gotten high and cleaned like a banshee, but now... Dirty dishes were piled in the sink, wine spilled down the counter... and Kit knew for a fact the bitch didn't have her half of the rent, again. They would've parted ways months ago if it wasn't Mia's name on the lease. Kit kicked a pair of nasty-ass panties out of her way. Gross. Legalities aside, they were still gonna have words.

No time to shower, and her uniform was still damp. She wished she could just change at the club, but if her laptop got nicked, she was screwed. HDL wouldn't cough one up on the company dime until she made junior analyst, which at the rate she was going would be another year, minimum.

Her phone buzzed, and she glanced at it. Mr. Asorav. He wanted to book her to walk Cecelia next week. The vamp's Teacup Pomeranian was definitely her favorite dog to hang out with, and the pay was stupid for spending time with the tiny pooch.

She smiled and texted back a thumbs up. Perfect. Quarter close would be done by then, and her asshole stalkers would steer clear; Manhattan was vamp territory. Too bad she couldn't afford to sanctify some place over there. Kit's dash of paranormal blood made her way too tempting a treat to hang out past sunset, and she had zero interest in becoming some vamp's thrall.

She glanced at the time. Shit, what she was gonna be was out of a job if she didn't hurry the hell up.

Five minutes later, she'd locked up the apartment and was clomping back down the steps in combat boots. Sweats covered up the trashy fishnets and booty shorts, and one of Chanté's massive hoodies was over the shredded T with the Club Skin logo.

She gripped her bag tighter as she rushed down the block, not usually nervous in this part of the city. Yeah, it was getting dark, but people were still out and about, all business as usual.

But for whatever reason, tonight felt different.

Might have something to do with her stalkers becoming bolder. Her steps slowed, one of them looming against a building near the entrance to the subway, arms crossed over his massive chest and leering. There was no mistaking he was waiting for her, his smile widening as she approached.

It wasn't a good look on him. Man was ugly as sin, shaggy black hair dusting over a face not even a mother would love. A dripping brand of a moon inside a pentagram was seared onto his forearm, and he was flaunting an MC cut—

Satan's Vengeance.

Oh, sweet baby Jesus. That was her psycho sperm donor's MC.

Her guts churned, head going light. She gripped her bag tighter, acting like she didn't give a fuck and wasn't totally freaking out inside.

Reaper had found her—

No, he's in jail for three years, eight months, and sixteen more days. You got this. It's a damned game. They're just fucking with you. Keep going.

She raised her chin and didn't break stride.

Her eyes flicked to the shifter's cut as she got closer. Patch read "Enforcer." Kit didn't doubt it. He looked like he could crush a parking meter in his meaty paws.

Damn it. Claymore had told her this would happen when she took the job at Skin. Had begged her to keep a low profile—

Her stalker blew her a wet kiss as she passed, and Kit gagged, her heart rate ticking up. But why the hell would her father's nasty ass shifter crew be down here? Just to torment her, or had Reaper sent them to haul her back upstate?

Nope. Not fucking happening.

She didn't see any of them on the subway, but she felt their eyes crawling over her. God, she was trapped in this fucking box… Her jaw clenched. *Prey, that's what they see you as. Don't give them the satisfaction. Stay cool.*

Hah! Stay cool…The urge to run intensified when the doors slid open at her stop. Kit's pulse raced, sweat sliding down her spine. On the platform a whip thin biker manspreading across a bench like a damned bad-boy romance novel ad licked his lips at her as she exited the train. Her steps faltered, commuters battering her as they passed. The biker stood, his eyes intent.

Holy fuck, he was coming towards her—

Screw being cool.

Kit bolted, sprinting up to street level. Skin was two blocks away, and she didn't stop running until she got there, swearing she heard them laughing behind her.

She collapsed on a bench in the employee changing area, head hanging between her knees and panting. Wiping away her tears. This was bad… so fucking bad…

The Enforcer, the bad boy in the subway… none of them had let her get a good look at them before. The last three weeks had started out with shadows glimpsed from the corner of her eye and that horrible feeling of being watched. Then the phone calls with some perv breathing heavy.

And the dead mice left at her door.

Claymore had said if she ever needed sanctuary…

But did she really trust anything he said?

She bit down on her lips. Not even a little.

And hello, running from shifters to be protected by shifters sounded pretty fucking stupid. What she needed was a shifter-free zone. Didn't they have those in Canada? Kit snorted. Even if they did, she wouldn't pass the DNA requirements for entry. Didn't matter if she hadn't gone through the change and never fucking would. Speciesist purists like her aunt didn't consider her human.

Fuck them.

She shoved her bag and sweats into her locker. Ugh. Kit scrubbed her hands over her face, sure she looked a mess. She couldn't go out there like this. She spent some time freshening her makeup in the mirror. Rubbing down her pits with hand soap. Rinse and repeat. Shifter assholes were probably getting off on the stink of her fear.

Goddamn it, they wouldn't take this away from her. Wouldn't force her into that box they'd put her mother in. She was more than a hole for their dicks.

She chucked the paper towels away and pushed through the doors, headed to the dance floor. Bass thumped, hot and heavy, everything else falling away. Kit's hips twitched to the beat. Accounting might pay the bills, but damn if she didn't feel this shit in her soul. The club's black lights flickered in time to the music, the crowd a writhing mass of bodies, letting go and inviting the now to pump through them.

For two nights a week, it was freedom, and Kit fucking loved it.

People cheered as she ascended the steps to her lucite podium. DJ Yhu pointed her finger at Kit in admonishment for being late, then grinned, spinning a new record. The Pretty Reckless blasted out over the techno beat.

Kit danced.

Booty shaking until her thighs trembled, grinding low and back up with a pop, hands sliding from her waist to the sides of her breast and burying in her hair, thrashing and wild with abandon.

Songs changed, and the energy built, sweat dripping between her breasts and slicking her thighs. The dip at the base of her spine channeling a steady stream downwards. Sal, one of the bartenders caught her eye and tapped his wrist. Two hours had already passed? Shit, she needed to take a break. Club mandated them after some dumb chick had passed out and fallen off her damned podium.

Kit still glared at him, and he laughed, holding up a bottle of water. Whatever. She sashayed down as the music morphed to a different beat and worked her way through the crowd. They had to be pushing maximum occupancy tonight.

"Looking good up there, Kit," Sal said, eye-fucking her as he passed her the bottle. Man had been trying to get in her pants since she auditioned last year.

Wasn't happening.

Yeah, he was hot with that scruffy square jaw and those baby blues, but men were off limits. All it would take was a kiss from someone with shifter genes to instigate the change.

Just a drop of saliva, semen, or blood, and she'd turn into one of those dirty fuckers.

No frickin' thank you.

Besides, it wasn't like any of them got her any hotter than she got herself. Batteries for the win.

She went to pull the bottle from his hand and Sal held on, a teasing grin tipping up his lips.

Kit let go. "You want it that bad you can have it, but you're not gonna be able to drool over my moves until I get one of those."

"Baby, you got no idea how bad I want it, and I'll drool over you any time you wanna show me those moves up close and personal. Trust me when I say, I will give it to you then."

She rolled her eyes and snatched the bottle from his hand.

He leaned against the bar, shoulders straining his black T. "Seriously Kit, when you gonna let me take you out?"

"You don't wanna take me out, you wanna Netflix and chill."

Sal smirked, watching her bring the water to her lips. "I wouldn't say no—"

"Then I'll do it for you." She batted her lashes at him and capped the bottle. "No."

"Baby, you're killing me!" He clutched at his chest and shook his head. "One day, you're gonna say yes. Meantime, Helena says Mia's in the ladies. You might wanna check that out before Sandoval catches wind of it."

Shit. Mia sticking her part of the rent up her nose was bad enough, but pissing where they both ate? Nuh uh. Girl needed a fucking intervention.

Again.

Kit left the main floor, grabbing her hoodie on the way. Last time she'd tried to save Mia from herself, they'd gotten into it and the girl had ripped Kit's T so bad her tits were hanging out. She couldn't afford to replace another one.

Or to keep covering the damned rent solo.

Bitches made a stink about Kit cutting the line to the ladies, but tough shit. They made a worse one when she flashed her uniform and told them it was temporarily closed. Mia was in a stall, her boots pointed knock-kneed beneath the metal divider.

Kit didn't bother being subtle about kicking out the bitches standing around gossiping like the fucking shitter was a coffeehouse. Her roomie needed to know what she was in for.

Mia decided to come out of the stall just as Kit cleared the room and threw the bolt on the door. Girl was a hot fucking mess, uniform hanging off her lank frame, blonde hair ratty, and smeared smokey cat-eye turning her eyes into pits.

She pinching at her nose, flashing a totally fake smile. "Hey—"

"Don't fucking even," Kit gritted out.

Mia was easily a foot taller, but that didn't stop Kit from grabbing her by the nape and hauling her skinny ass against the sinks. Girl's pupils were huge, and her left nostril sported a crusty red ring.

Kit slammed on the water and shoved her face into it. "You need to clean the fuck up."

"What the hell!" Mia protested, trying to wriggle away.

"Exactly what I was thinking. You want this job? 'Cause I want this job, and if someone sees a strung-out dancer in a Skin uniform doing blow in the bathroom, you think Sandoval won't catch wind? He'll fire your ass and mine too for covering for you."

"He won't"—Mia sputtered—"it's not—"

"Fuck your excuses and what it is or isn't. This is the last goddamned time I'm doing this. Next time, I'll hand your ass over to him myself!"

Kit let go, and Mia collapsed to the floor, sobbing. "You don't understand—"

"Nope, I'm done with trying to do that and well into not

giving a fuck." Kit held out her palm, the other on her cocked hip. "Hand it over."

Mia's jaw set. Oh, hell fucking no. Kit fisted her hair, dragging her roomie over the piss splattered tiles to a stall, kicking and screaming. "I told you I ain't playin'; you won't hand it over, you can flush it yourself."

"Ow! Kit, stop!" Mia's face knocked against the toilet seat and she gagged.

Served the bitch fucking right. Kit was so goddamned done with this shit—"Flush it!"

Mia's cheek cracked against the seat again. "Ow! Fuck! Fine!"

A sad little baggy plunked into the bowl, and Kit kicked the lever with her boot, sending it down. She dropped her roomie, pretty sure that living situation was at an end, totally fucking disgusted. "Now clean your ass up, and you better be out of here by the time I get outta this damned stall." She retreated into one of them, slamming it shut and waiting for it.

Didn't take long.

"You know what?" Mia scrambled off the floor. "Fuck this job and fuck you, Kit! You're such a fucking ungrateful cunt after I took your nasty, half-breed ass in. And you're right, this is the last fucking time. I want you and all your shit outta my apartment tonight, or it's gonna be on the street!"

The door slammed, and Kit sat on the bowl, shaking.

She wouldn't fucking cry.

She could handle this. Figure out some place to land. Wouldn't let those shifter fucks know how they were getting to her—

You got this, girl.

She wiped away a tear. She didn't fucking have it. Not even a little.

The door to the hall opened, and women started filtering

in again, voicing their "what the fucks" and "did you see that's." Kit stared up at the ceiling, blinking back tears.

You're gonna be fine. Don't let them get to you.

I won't be fine, and I'm scared as fuck.

They don't know that. Fake it till you make it, shit will come true someday.

"Hey! You can't—"

Great. What the fuck now? Kit wiped her cheeks again, prepping herself to face the owner of the indignant voice. The vapid chatter on the other side of the stall door cut off. Kit's eyes narrowed at a pair of man's big ass shit-kickers strutting into the room. The women at the sink scattered, and the other stalls cleared out like it was a fire drill at the hiss of his zipper dropping.

Are you fucking serious?

Kit flushed out of habit and slammed open the stall door.

A man built like a Viking god stood at the sink. Shaggy blonde hair kissed his collar. He had to be six four and the shoulders on him made her mouth go dry... so did the patch on the back of his cut.

The Maw of Mayhem MC.

Had Claymore sent him down for her? Kit eyed the way his ass filled out his jeans, suspecting there were worse body-guards to—

Sweet baby Jesus, asshole was pissing in the sink.

Kit sidled up to the one beside him and started washing her hands. She bit her lip, focused on being hygienic, not checking out his crown piercing. Nope.

Yeah, that was a lie, but whatever.

He glanced down at her through messy strands of wheaten blond hair, stubbled lips pursing as he looked her over like she was a buffet.

Game on.

Oh, hell no. Fuck this biker asshole. "You know that's not a urinal, right?" she asked, glaring at him in the mirror. This one's cut read Vice Prez. No wonder he was so fucking arrogant, coming in here and doing his business in the sink.

Kit flicked her eyes from his cut to his face, and quicksilver grey eyes trapped hers.

Oh, girl… get you some…

His throat bobbed, and he tucked himself away. "Desperate times."

Goddamn, his voice was low and rumbly and the thought of him whispering dirty, nasty things in her ear soaked her panties clean through.

He barked out a laugh like he knew it.

Fucking shifters. Kit reached past him to slap on the water in his sink, rinsing it down. "That's fucking disgusting. You need to leave before I call security."

He grinned, a dimple slicing down his left cheek as he stepped too close to her. Did he think he was gonna intimidate her? She put her hands on her hips and scowled, not about to move a damned inch.

He wet his lips, and his hand came up, stroking down the side of her cheek. Kit's pulse raced, wanting to lean into that touch so damned bad. She gritted her teeth at the unfamiliar desire.

No.

Not. Fucking. Happening. Her hand snaked up to grab his wrist, and her breath caught, a jolt of electricity zinging through her. Every little hair on his wrist igniting her palm like a fuse, heat rushing through her body to detonate between her thighs.

He inhaled, his pupils blowing out as his chest rose.

Kit's breath caught, then stuttered out, her brows creasing. What the fuck was that about? Nope. Didn't care. Fuckboy had to go. "D-don't touch me."

"Stop wanting me to," he murmured, tilting up her mouth to his.

Goddamn, she so wanted him to—

Get a fucking grip! He's a shifter!

Her fist took him in the jaw, and he stumbled back, looking shocked as hell—

—Nope. He looked like he was about to eat her.

She bolted for the door—

Gunshots.

People in the hall freaked the fuck out, making for the emergency exit. The rush pushed Kit back into the bathroom, and the shifter caught her before she fell. He cradled her against him, and damn, the man was stacked—

And a fucking a shifter.

Kit still had the worst urge to throw her arm around his neck and bury her face in his neck.

No.

She wriggled away, and he slammed the door shut and locked it, his breath coming fast. He ran a hand down his face, head back against the wall. His throat looked damp, like he was sweating. What was that about? Was whoever out there—

Kit's eyes widened. Oh shit. Satan's Vengeance had been following her, and this guy was from the Maw of Mayhem. The two MCs were bitter rivals. The whole fucked-up war between Claymore and Reaper was what stole Kit's mother from her and gotten her shuffled off to her crazy-ass aunt's.

The two MCs had ruined her goddamned life once, and it looked like they were back for round two.

The biker checked his phone, then raked a hand through his shaggy blond hair and pulled out a gun. Kit swallowed the lump in her throat. Yeah, that's definitely what this was, and that man shouldn't be so goddamned hot when he was about to commit murder.

She moved back against the far wall, and his head swiveling to look at her. He rocked his jaw, fingering where she'd slugged him, his eyes traveling down her body. That flush of heat went through her again, and she squeezed her thighs together.

"Don't even think about it, asshole," she gritted out, eyeing his gun.

He smirked, shifting his cock. Yeah, she was pretty sure he was thinking about it. So was she, damn it. Her nipples had beaded up so tight they ached.

A frown crossed his chiseled brow, and raised his gun, turning back to the door like he was gonna open it. She hadn't even registered how quiet it'd gotten.

He glanced back at her, that quicksilver gaze trapping her again. "Stay here."

She rolled her eyes, crossing her arms over her chest. Yeah, like that was gonna happen. He licked his lips, following the motion, then turned away, easing open the door—

Fuck this.

Kit burst out from behind him and was through the emergency exit before the bathroom door slammed against the wall.

She'd jumped the turnstile and was shaking in the subway car, getting ogled by a bunch of randos before she realized she'd left her bag at the club.

She couldn't go back. Couldn't.

Calm down. Make a plan.

A plan. Right. She didn't have another phone, but Claymore had made her get a second ID, and she didn't carry the keys to her hatchback. Those were at the apartment... which she was probably locked out of, unless Mia was home. Bitch would let her in, right? Yeah. She wanted her gone; she'd let her get her stuff.

Kit ran a hand through her hair. It was gonna be okay. It had to be. She got off at the next stop, making herself walk the rest of the way home. The lack of eyes on her sent a shiver up her spine, wondering what'd happened to that biker from the bathroom. Her chest ached at the thought of him getting hurt.

Kit pounded on the apartment door, but Mia wasn't there. Fuck… The super was a stone cold bitch, but what choice did she have? Kit went down to the first floor, wiping her sweaty palms down her thighs.

Mrs. Petrinko was not fucking pleased to see her. Woman gripped her housecoat tight to her throat, shooing cats back inside and lecturing at Kit about decent hours, respectable women, and throwing in a "where's my money, bitch?" before giving Kit the spare.

Just another day in the life.

Kit packed up her stuff on auto pilot. Wasn't like she had a ton, though you wouldn't know it as she threw her weight against her shitty maroon hatchback's passenger door to close it. She stepped back, looking at her wadded-up life shoved inside. She swept away the trickling moisture on her cheek, rounding to the driver's side.

The scuff of a footstep echoed through the underground vault, and Kit looked across the parking garage.

A long, lean shadow separated itself from one of the distant pillars by the exit, stopping just shy of coming into the light.

Kit saw enough.

Her breath caught, heart in her throat. Lank salt and pepper hair framed the man's hatchet face, shadows turning his eyes to black voids. He shoved his hands into his pockets, and his grin sliced ear to ear.

"Run little mouse…"

Her keys bit into her palm, blood frozen cold. Kit's back hit the driver's side door, hand scrabbling behind her for the handle. Nope. It wasn't. Couldn't be. Asshole was still locked up…

The keys were in the ignition, and she slammed into reverse—

The man was gone.

Her heart thudded in her chest, fingers checking the locks, hatchback creeping past the rows of cars. Nobody in sight.

He's in jail, Kit. Your father's in jail.

Right. God, she was being stupid. She'd get notice if Reaper was up for parole, and Claymore would've given her a heads up. He hadn't said shit about it when he'd called last week.

Her grip on the wheel relaxed.

A homeless guy was camped out on the sidewalk when she pulled onto the street. Kit snorted. That was probably who she'd seen, only imagined that gravelly deep woods twang… Yeah, that was it. Everything tonight had put her on edge. She'd tell Chanté all about it when she got to her place, and her bestie would laugh her ass off…

Kit chewed her lip, waiting for the light to change, wishing she had her phone.

What if Claymore had been at the club?

She laughed. It was probably too much to ask for the two MCs to pop each other off and leave her the hell alone… a visual of that biker from the bathroom flashed through her mind. Okay, maybe not him.

He'd probably be there if you took Clay up on his offer of sanctuary…

Yeah, and that was just another reason not to go. She hadn't ever experienced that level of temptation, and sacrificing her humanity wasn't her definition of safety.

Kit circled Chanté's block six times before a parking space opened up, then sat there staring out the windshield.

Why was all this shit happening to her? Kit teared up again, swearing. Why couldn't she ever seem to catch a goddamned break?

What doesn't kill you makes you stronger.

Kit snorted. As someone who'd almost been murdered by her own damned blood, she could safely say that platitude was bullshit... and now here she was, on the fucking run again.

There had to be more to life than this.

She killed the engine, anger sweeping in to replace the sadness. Done with Mia's bullshit, done with being afraid of her father's damn shadow, and done with fucking Claymore James.

There *was* more to life than this, and she'd be damned if she wasn't coming for it.

NEXT IN THE SERIES

Want to find out what happened at the club and how Kit fits into Grim's story? Check out the next installment in the series:

———

Bass thumped, heavy and hot, throbbing up through the soles of Grim's shit kickers. The club's black lights flickered with the beat, highlighting the sweat-slicked bodies undulating in a writhing mass of lust and abandon below him.

He leaned back against the balcony's bar, vibing enough "don't fuck with me" to keep all but the brain-dead sluts off him. Not that he could blame them, but he didn't tend to stick his dick in stupid.

Or anything else.

—laughing—

Happy about that, you furry motherfucker?

Fucking cat was out of control. Grim scanned the pit of simmering sex below, the stink of human desire thick in his nose. He turned to his alpha, not fucking impressed, or in the mood for bullshit.

"This is what we rode five hours for?"

Clay gave a slow nod, more closed-lipped than usual, totally fixated on one of the lucite pillars rising up from the dance floor. Grim shook his head and took another sip of his over-priced beer. Clay'd spill when he was ready and not a moment before. There had to be a damned good reason for them to be there, and if he wanted to stare at an empty platform, more power to him. The others had plenty of eye candy to enjoy.

And human or not, those dancers could move, their get-ups not leaving much to the imagination. Fishnets, booty shorts, and shredded Ts reading "Skin" straining across their tits as they worked the poles in the center of each platform.

But as much as he approved on principle, his dick couldn't care less.

[SMUG]

Fuck his cat and this shit. He downed the last of his beer and cracked the glass onto the bar.

"Gotta piss."

Grim shouldered past, and Clay grunted, still fixated on that platform. Whatever had caught the alpha's attention had brought his cat close to the surface. He wasn't going anywhere.

Grim pushed through the crowd, shrugging off roaming hands and bodies pressing close. Whispered promises and innuendo fell on deaf ears. One brazen stolen kiss, and a tongue laced with the tang of a narcotic tangled with his. He spun the woman back into the throng and spat.

Hall for the john was packed, moans coming from the men's room. He shouldered past the line for the ladies, through the door.

"Hey! You can't—"

Yeah, he could. A dozen stalls, all closed. Wide eyes watching him in the mirror, lipstick and mascara dropping, their owners scurrying back like vermin. Gasping as he unzipped and started pissing into the sink. Grim's head tipped back with a long exhale. Fuuuck—

A flush and slam of a stall door opening. The water in the sink beside him crashed on. He glanced over. A petite, raven-haired woman dressed like the podium dancers beneath a man's oversized, unzipped hoodie soaped up her hands. Grim pursed his lips at her sinful curves. God freaking damn…

"You know that's not a urinal, right?" she asked, her reflection glaring at him in the mirror.

Or more accurately, glaring at his cut.

Her whiskey dark eyes flicked up and met his. Grim's mouth went dry. His dick twitched as he shoved it back into his jeans. She didn't drop her gaze.

"Desperate times." Grim's voice rumbled, his inner beast sitting up and taking notice, along with his cock. *Are you fucking kidding me?*

—want—

Now, you want? He barked out a laugh. The shit on that chick's tongue must've been a premium grade miracle.

Little miss five-foot-nothing-and-not-into-bikers reached past him to slap on the water in his sink, rinsing it down. "That's fucking disgusting. You need to leave before I call security."

Damn, she was a live one.

Grim crowded into her space, and she didn't budge, glaring up at him with her hands on her hips, just begging for him to smack that ass. He wet his lips and stroked down the side of her cheek, trailing to her quickening pulse. Her hand snaked up to grab his wrist, and a jolt went through him, cock kicking against his zipper.

The ebony of her pupils blew out, eating away the warmth of her irises. The scent of her arousal flooded his nose. Her breath caught, then stuttered out, a little crease appearing between her brows. "D-don't touch me."

"Stop wanting me to," he murmured, tilting up her mouth to his.

Her fist took him in the jaw and he stumbled back. The fuck?

—YESSS—

Within, his beast coiled to pounce as she flung open the bathroom door, storming out—

Gunshots.

Clay.

Grim's cat scrabbled to get out. The beast's consciousness slammed into his, overwhelming him with the desire to shift and charge through the crowd, rending and tearing until he—

The hallway erupted with people frantic to escape, and the woman fell back into the bathroom. He lunged forward to steady her, the press of her body against his distracting the beast long enough to wrestle back control. She wriggled away, and Grim slammed the door shut and locked it, panting.

Shit, that was close…

[ANGER]

We're not shifting here. He needed to think, not react, goddamn it. He pulled his cell, then shoved it back into his pocket. Fuck. They'd ridden down alone. MC wouldn't be able to back them up for hours. He raked a hand through his shaggy blond hair and pulled his piece, listening for a break in the deluge of bodies streaming past the door.

Movement to his right. The woman had flattened herself against the far wall. Grim rocked his jaw. She had one hell of a hook, and a set of legs to match. Damned if they weren't tight as fuck…

"Don't even think about it, asshole," she gritted out, eyeing his gun.

Grim smirked, shifting his cock. Oh, he was thinking about it all right. Her peaked nipples and the way she rubbed her thighs together said he wasn't the only one.

—Clay—

Right. Wasn't the fucking time. Head in the game. The rush outside the door had dissipated and Grim raised his gun, fingers on the doorknob. He glanced back at her.

"Stay here."

She rolled her eyes, arms crossed over what had to be all natural DDs.

Goddamn.

—want—

Later. He eased open the door and slid—

She burst out from behind him and was gone before the door slammed against the wall. A smile tipped up his lips, his proverbial tail twitching. Any other situation, he'd chase that down and tag it. Fucking figured he and his cat would agree on something now.

The hall was deserted, a lone cocktail napkin fluttering abandoned in the pulsing lights. Grim's jaw clenched, the shit music drowning out any sounds from the balcony above. His finger inched towards the trigger, the dusky scent of cat edging out the reek of humanity in the room.

Mother. Fucker.

He crept up the stairs to the balcony—

"I done told you what would happen, Claymore, laying rights on what ain't yours to claim. Destiny always takes its due."

Grim's foot paused on the last step, his stomach dropping at the gravely deep woods drawl. No— Asshole had close to four more years in the pen—

"Fuck you." Clay gritted out, his voice racked with pain.

"Mmm, think I'll fuck that ol' lady of yours instead. Heard Marie ain't much for conversatin' these days, but I ain't never been real interested in what she had t'say."

Grim ducked into an alcove behind the curtain of the VIP section. Swearing and a scuffle sounded over the pounding techno beat, then the sharp crack of flesh on flesh.

Man laughed at Clay's agonized groan. "Easy… knock that blade free, an' you'll ruin the scene. Let's stretch this out a tic. Shiv, kill that godawful shit."

A semi-automatic fired and the music cut out, the silence a deafening void.

Grim nosed the dusky velvet curtain aside with the barrel of his gun, peeking through. Cold sweat drenched his body, cat trying to tuck tail. He fought to kill the whine scrabbling to burst from his insides. Wishing like hell his eyes hadn't confirmed what his churning guts already knew.

Reaper was out.

[FEAR]

Yeah. They were fucked. Totally fucking fucked.

Across the room, a half dozen brothers from their rival MC, Satan's Vengeance, were raiding the bar with one eye on the show. Grapple, Reaper's enforcer, had Clay on his knees, one massive hand ripping the alpha's head back to bare the his throat.

The other was on a silver knife buried to the hilt in Clay's shoulder.

That son of a bitch.

Grim swallowed bile, shoving away the memory of that burn. Black fire webbing decay through his flesh, paralyzing his beast—

—run—

No. Let me think. Shit was easier said than done, but— how'd they know to hit them at the club tonight?

Unless the MC had a rat… or a Mouse. Fucking tech nerd was supposed to be keeping tabs on the prison.

Anger stilled the tremor in his hand, and Grim blinked the sweat from his eyes. Because if Reaper and his brothers were here, they hadn't just been betrayed by one of their own, they'd been offered up on a silver fucking platter as sacrifices.

How the hell had the psycho prick gotten out?

The lanky biker sniffed, running a hand under his nose. Grim tensed at the smirk tipping up the asshole's lips, keenly aware of the stink of his own fear. Reaper snagged a bottle from one of his boys. His rings clanked against the glass as he imbibed, that icy blue gaze, dead as a skittering leaves, sweeping the shadows—

—until it met Grim's.

Reaper's lips twitched again. "Ah. Now that we're all here—"

He raised his gun and blew away half of Clay's skull.

———

Want more?

Click here to get the next installment, available February 2, 2024:

GRIMDARKE

And sign up for my newsletter to be the first to know when the next books in the Maw of Mayhem MC Series are released!

https://aknevermore.com/

BOOKS BY AK NEVERMORE

THE DAE DIARIES - URBAN FANTASY WITH SPICE

One Night in Bliss — *FREE TO READ*

Flame & Shadow

Air & Darkness — (August 2024)

Playing with Fire — *FREE TO READ* (October 2024)

THE PRICE OF TALENT - STEAMY DARK SCI-FI ROMANTASY

Breeder — *FREE TO READ*

Breaker

Destroyer — *FREE TO READ (August 2024)*

Binder — (September 2024)

Split — (November 2024)

Overlord — (January 2024)

THE MAW OF MAYHEM - PARANORMAL MC EROTICA

Bites of Mayhem — *FREE TO READ*

The Maw of Mayhem — *FREE TO READ*

Grimdarke

Darker

Kit-Kat

Katherine — *(Forthcoming)*

ACKNOWLEDGMENTS

Thank YOU so much for downloading my book. I hope you enjoyed reading it as much as I enjoyed writing it, and if you've got some time, please consider rating it on Goodreads:

Rate The Maw of Mayhem on Goodreads

To Lenore and the Betas swimming around in my fishbowl, you all have my most heartfelt thanks. Your feedback pushes me to be better and sends me down rabbit holes I might not have otherwise fallen into.

And the biggest thanks to Mr. Nevermore. I couldn't have done any of this without your belief in my dreams, or without you keeping the party going with the ravens while I'm wandering about Wonderland.

ABOUT THE AUTHOR

AK Nevermore writes science fiction and urban fantasy. She enjoys operating heavy machinery, freebases coffee, and gives up sarcasm for Lent every year.

A Jane-of-all-trades, she's a certified chef, restores antiques, and dabbles in beekeeping when she's not reading voraciously or running down the dream in her beat-up camo Chucks.

Unable to ignore the voices in her head, and unwilling to become medicated, she writes full time. Her books explore dark worlds, perversely irreverent and profound, and always entertaining.

Want more Nevermore?
Sign up for her newsletter and never miss a release!

Nevermore News

Cover design by Bookmojo

Digital ISBN: 979-8-9887464-1-6

Print ISBN: 978-1-964466-03-3